CLASH

MELANIE STANFORD

INTRODUCTION

Planning a party is easy, falling in love is hard.

No longer content to be a Los Angeles socialite, Elizabeth Elliot starts her own party planning business: **Excessively Diverted**, making dreams come true one party at a time. She even knows how to handle those unruly party guests, like Antonio Reyes, the man who drank too much, insulted the décor, and didn't know the difference between crudités and canapés. The nerve.

So when this same Tony Reyes demands she plan his daughter's Sweet Sixteen, Elizabeth refuses, no matter how many dollar signs are attached to his name. That is until Elizabeth discovers her new business is in trouble. She must suck up her pride and work with Tony, despite how much she hates the man.

As Elizabeth gets to know Tony and his daughter, her clear-cut hatred starts to get muddled with *feelings*—the kind that could screw up the job, and her life, completely. She must decide whether risking her heart is worth it…

But who has time for all that when there's a party to be planned?

Cover by Gabrielle Prendergast
Digital ISBN: 978-0-9959153-2-9
Print ISBN: 978-0-9959153-3-6

To Coralie and Natalie
Sisters I don't get to see often
But who I love more than Beth loves Ava and Mari

CHAPTER 1

I never thought I'd say this, but I love my job. I bring smiles to people's faces. I make them laugh, dance, weep. Their dreams come true thanks to me. I'm like a frickin' fairy godmother.

No, a fairy godmother is always old, fat, or both. I'm a dream come true.

"The party is amazing," June said to me, her eyes surveying the room. "Better than I ever could have hoped." She took one of my hands in hers. "You've saved my life, Elizabeth Elliot."

That's me—the party-planning angel, saving lives one center-piece at a time. That should've been my brand line. Too late to change my logo?

My gaze caught on a vase that was off-center. "Excuse me, June," I said, pulling my hand from her leathery grip. I never wanted to get old. Wrinkles were gross. "I have a disaster to avert. Enjoy your party. And don't worry about a thing."

Her gratitude echoed over the string quartet, but I didn't stay to listen. I searched the ballroom for Juliet. If she didn't get her tiny behind in gear, she'd be *so* fired. Which I told her once I found her by the bar, working out a problem with the ice. Honestly, who has problems with ice?

"I'm so sorry," Juliet said about the vase, "I'll get on it right away."

She scurried away, her jet-black hair in a perfect bun, not one strand out of place. Her gray skirt and jacket were both wrinkle free, and she didn't wobble one bit on those stilettos. Honestly, I would never fire Juliet—she was the best assistant I'd ever had. Just contemplating interviews with another string of idiots set my teeth on edge—but she didn't need to know that. I'd learned, in the few short weeks she'd worked for me, that Juliet functioned much better under pressure.

"Stop shoving them in my face!" a voice said nearby. "I don't want another tacky crudité."

Tacky? TACKY? I spun toward the voice. Two men stood by the bar, one holding a plate piled high with canapés, NOT crudités. He was happily munching while the other was sipping champagne, his nose wrinkling as if his glass of Moët & Chandon smelled bad.

"These are delicious," the first man said. He was probably forty-ish, blond, and slightly chubby. There was a smear of something white on his cheek.

The other man was tall and slim, his blue suit perfectly cut across the shoulders. "I'll take your word for it," he said. His voice had a slight accent, but I couldn't place it.

The chubby one waved a canapé around. "You have to taste it."

"Stig, if you put that thing in my face again, I will shove it up your nose."

My hands went to my hips. Oh no, there would be no fights at one of my parties.

"What is your problem, Tony?" Stig asked.

"My problem is that I was dragged to yet another showy and tasteless display of wealth, with nothing to make it the slightest bit amusing or worthwhile."

Anger lit my entire body on fire.

"The pretentious string quartet, décor that looks like it came from my grandmother's living room, food that's hardly edible, and the same old people talking about the same old things."

"I think you've had enough to drink for one evening." Stig reached for Tony's champagne.

Tony knocked it back before his friend could take it, then whistled loudly for a waiter.

I marched over. He would calm down or get out.

He saw me approaching, his expression of annoyance didn't budge. He held out the glass for me to take, as if I was some kind of servant.

"Do I look like a waiter to you?" I demanded.

His eyes swept me from top to bottom. "Not interested."

My eyes narrowed. "Excuse me?"

"Whatever it is you want, I am not interested. I don't want to talk, I don't want to flirt, I don't want to date. If you're not going to get me another drink, then you can go away."

His friend, Stig, choked on his drink.

He went to move past me but I stepped in his way. "Tony, is it?" I didn't wait for him to respond. "Believe me, I don't want to date you either."

He pressed his hand to his chest in mock hurt.

"You need to step outside and take a breather."

He leaned in and I caught a whiff of alcohol mixed with cologne. He was tall, but so was I, especially when I raised my chin to meet his gaze. "Who the hell are you to tell me what to do?"

My eyes flashed. "This is my party, which makes me God, and you the mere mortal who has to obey my wishes."

He leaned back. "So you are the help."

"I am not—"

"I need a drink." He slid past me, grabbing another from the nearest tray.

No one was allowed to interrupt me. I scanned the party, making sure our interaction hadn't caused a disturbance. He'd rattled me, but I would not be unprofessional.

I followed him, lightly grabbing his elbow.

He stopped, tilting his head at me. "You again."

I gave him my nicest, most polite, smile. "If you cause a scene,"

I said, my voice low, "I will have you ejected from this party." I patted his arm. To anyone watching, it probably did look like we were flirting.

He guzzled another glass of champagne then smiled at me. "It would be fun to call your bluff. Liven up this fiesta."

"How do you know June?"

He blinked at my change in subject. "Her husband, Harold, is a client of mine."

"And how do you think Harold would feel if you ruined his wife's party? I can't imagine he'd be pleased."

Tony shifted his feet and avoided my eyes.

"I don't know what you do," I said, "but I've never met a businessman who likes losing a client."

"And you're an expert?" He took a shot. A couple more of those and he'd be getting into a fistfight with someone.

I placed my hands on his cheeks, forcing him to look at me. Anyone watching would've thought I was just being friendly. Hopefully. "I think you've had enough for one night. This is your last warning."

His jaw clenched. "Out of all the women I have ever met, I think I hate you most of all."

My smile was tight-lipped. "The feeling is mutual."

He stalked away, and I immediately went in search of Juliet.

"Watch that one," I said, pointing to Tony in the crowd. He was sitting at a table with his friend Stig. "Let me know if he gets out of hand."

"Will do," Juliet replied.

A few hours later, the awful Tony had left—luckily without causing a scene—and the party started to wind down. It had been a smashing success. Obviously.

June thanked me a zillion times for making the evening more than she imagined. The new caterer I'd decided to take a chance on had been sublime—proving once again my intuition was spot-on. And Juliet hadn't let me down once.

Other than the blip that was Tony, it was a stellar night.

CHAPTER 2

THE NEXT MORNING, I SAT AT THE BREAKFAST TABLE NURSING A COFFEE and a headache. Despite the party's success, I'd tossed and turned the entire night.

"How did it go last night, honey?" my dad asked.

I rubbed circles into my temples. "Almost perfect."

"You're too hard on yourself." Dad was checking his reflection in a handheld mirror. He lifted the skin underneath his eyebrow.

"You don't need a lift." I snatched the mirror from his hand and checked my own reflection. I needed some eye cream stat before my appointment today. It was a consultation for a Sweet Sixteen party and I couldn't look old and unhip in front of a teenage girl.

"Almost perfect." Dad sighed, eyeing the mirror I'd confiscated, as if it would show him something new next time he looked.

I stood and circled the table, leaning over his shoulder and putting the mirror in his face. "You *are* perfect." My sister Mari liked to tell me how ridiculous it was that I still lived at home, but Dad needed me. Plus, I loved our Malibu beach house.

"My party though…" Everything had gone smoothly, aside from that minor disturbance which I would not dwell on. I couldn't control everything, couldn't account for people.

Dad placed the mirror face down on the table. "I'm sure it was lovely, Elizabeth." He grabbed my hand, his skin baby soft despite the wrinkles.

"It was." I patted his hand. "But I haven't reached perfection yet. I'll get there."

I had never wanted to work. Once high school ended I had every intention of being the quintessential socialite. Shopping, parties, men. Red carpet events and paparazzi. Okay, the paparazzi had been scarce. If I lived in New York, they would've been following my every move I'm sure, but here in LA they were more interested in the actresses and models and reality stars. At one point, I'd sunk so low I pitched a reality show idea to a studio exec my dad knew, but he wasn't interested in my life. The nerve. Not that I would've done it anyway. To parade myself in front of cameras 24/7? As if.

But the last few years had begun to feel empty and boring. Pointless. I had watched both my younger sisters get married before me—Mari even had kids, not that I wanted to go there. Ava went to college, not that I wanted to do that either. She performed with orchestras and The Eric Wentworth Band. She married someone famous—*the* Eric Wentworth himself. I was the one who was supposed to marry the famous man.

Even if I didn't want the same things they did, I yearned for more.

Not that I didn't love my father, and my life. But it became...not enough.

And then I planned this fabulous party. The theme had been the movie *Pillow Talk*, and people gossiped about it for months. There was an article about it in the LA Times. A month later, one of dad's friends, who'd been at the *Pillow Talk* party, asked me if I'd be interested in planning her son's graduation party. I almost said no, until I saw the amount she was willing to pay me. So I took the job. Much to my surprise, I loved it. I was *proud* of myself. After that, Dad helped me rent a space for my new office, I hired a decorator and my first assistant, and **Excessively Diverted** was born. I never realized I could get paid to do something so fun.

"I better get going," I said to Dad. "I don't want to be late for my meeting."

"I've got an appointment with my trainer," he said. "Lunch at The Ivy later?"

I planted a kiss on his cheek. "I'll call you if my meeting goes over." I headed to the stairs, planning my outfit for the day.

"Knock 'em dead," Dad said behind me.

I didn't bother turning around. "I always do."

My office was small, which I hated, but classic, which I loved. The floors were dark wood, the walls a rich cream, and the accents all silvers and purples. It was the perfect mix of warm and cool— exactly how I saw myself.

Juliet was on the phone when I walked in.

"You'll have to give me a better idea of what you're looking for before I bring it to Miss Elliot." She handed me a latte, still warm. No matter when I came into the office, she always had a warm latte waiting for me. I had no clue how she did it but I didn't need to know, I just needed my warm latte. "I'm afraid Miss Elliot doesn't take on projects with such a low budget. No, she would never agree. I'm sorry…"

This was why I needed Juliet. To screen out the rustics and hill-billies so I wouldn't have to deal with them myself.

At my desk, I flipped through the Sweet Sixteen portfolio I'd created. Pages and pages of different themes and designs. There had to be something in here that would work. The girl's father was some tycoon or CEO or something. Actually, I had no clue what he did, only that he was rich. Rolling in it, million-dollar, money-clip type rich. When Juliet had handed me the message a few days ago, detailing who he was and what he wanted, she'd written three dollar signs by his name—her way of telling me this was a client I wanted—no *needed*—to land.

My phone rang. "Mr. Reyes and Miss Reyes are here to see you," Juliet said.

"Send them in." I adjusted my blouse, quickly checked my lipstick, snapping the compact closed when Juliet opened my office door.

"Mr. Reyes, Miss Reyes, this is Elizabeth Elliot." She motioned them inside then went back to her desk.

I stood, my smile freezing to a grimace.

Mr. Reyes paused in the doorway. His face went from confusion, to recognition, and to—dare I say—embarrassment? Shame? Full-on mortification and repentance?

His eyebrows lowered. "Miss Elliot?"

"Yes, I am Elizabeth Elliot, owner of **Excessively Diverted**." I held my hand out for him to shake. "It's very nice to meet you, Tony." Sarcasm dripped from my words, I didn't bother to disguise it.

The daughter, who had been in the process of pulling out the chair, stilled. Her eyes flicked back and forth between us.

He made no move to enter the room. "I didn't realize…"

I almost bit my tongue, but what was the point? There was no way I was landing this client, not after the way we'd clashed last night. I didn't want the job now, no matter how many dollar signs were beside Tony Reyes' name.

"Would you have been more polite?" I asked. "Better behaved, perhaps?"

Miss Reyes gaped. "Dad! What did you do?"

He didn't even have the grace to flush. Or respond.

I took a deep breath, pointedly ignoring Tony Reyes. "I apologize, Miss Reyes. As much as I would have enjoyed making your Sweet Sixteen everything you could have hoped, I'm afraid your father does not care for my tastes. I'm sorry that you wasted your time coming down here."

I sat back down at my desk and proceeded to shuffle through papers, trying to look busy. A clear dismissal.

"Who do you think you are that you can kick me out of your office?"

What a snob. I might not have had as much money as he did, but that didn't mean I wasn't *someone*. "I am Elizabeth Elliot, and like you so obviously pointed out—this is *my* office. Who I choose to meet with, or not, is my decision."

His eyes flashed. "You—"

"Dad!" The daughter hissed something at her father, something that sounded like "fix this," before stomping from the room.

Tony's whole face had reddened. He closed his eyes.

Smirking, I leaned back in my chair. This would be *oh so good*. I didn't know why his daughter wanted me in particular, but I could tell he would do what she wanted. Which meant grovelling. Yes, there would definitely be grovelling.

I waited. He hadn't opened his eyes. Was he counting to ten? Or a hundred?

My smirk was in place when he finally looked at me. His jaw clenched.

"I drank too much last night."

I waited. That couldn't be his apology.

Tony eyed me. I didn't blink. I'd perfected the art of getting what I wanted when I was seven years old and I hadn't lost the technique. It was a matter of not backing down.

"I didn't mean what I said."

"Yes, you did."

He folded his arms over his chest defensively. "Okay, I did, but—"

"Are you really going to insult me again?"

"Are you capable of not talking so I can finish? I—"

"No." I folded my hands over my desk. "I'm sorry for your daughter's sake, but there is no way we will be able to work together, and nothing you can say will change that. Please leave before you waste any more of my time."

Tony came to the edge of my desk, fisting his hands on top and leaning toward me. "I booked an appointment. You agreed to meet with me and I'm not leaving."

I stood up, unwilling to give him that power over me. "You made your opinion on my taste and skills apparent last night. I can't imagine why you would want to use my services." He opened his mouth but I didn't let him speak. "Even if you do like what I put together, you're probably incapable of being anything other than a pompous jerk who can't see farther than his gold cufflinks. You'd need an entire personality makeover before I would ever agree to work with you."

He had no response. He actually seemed taken aback.

"You can see yourself out."

I didn't watch him leave, but I heard the door close behind him, the tension in the room evaporating with one click.

CHAPTER 3

Venting to my father at lunch wasn't enough. He'd listened, said all the right things, but there'd been a cloud over his eyes as if he was worried about something else. I finally quit talking, not wanting to stress Dad out.

But I was still simmering over Tony Reyes. The nerve he had, demanding I meet with him despite his insults. Pulling the, "who do you think you are?" bit with me, as if he was too important for me to deny. So I didn't have pockets as deep, but I wouldn't work with that man if he paid me a billion dollars.

When I got into my car after lunch, I called Ava.

"Hey Beth, what's up?" she said on the other end.

"I met this guy and he makes me want to scream."

"You like him then."

"Ha ha ha. That's not funny."

"Who is this guy?"

In the background, I could hear the voices of kids laughing, calling out to each other. "Are you in the middle of class?"

"No, but it's almost the end of the lunch hour."

I waved that away. "He almost ruined an event I threw, and

then today he marched into my office demanding I plan a party for his daughter."

"Yikes."

"Is that all you have to say?" Ava could've given me more than 'yikes,' she was my sister after all.

"I'm sure you handled him," she said. Did I detect a note of disapproval in her tone?

"I did. And he deserved everything he got." And more.

"Beth. What did you do?"

"Stop being so judgy. I was a complete professional."

There was silence on the other end. She didn't believe me. The nerve!

"It's just…"

"Spit it out, Ava."

"**Excessively Diverted** is still kind of a new business, right? I would imagine word of mouth has a big influence on most of your clients. You don't want some guy, as jerky as he was, to go around telling people you're…"

My eyes narrowed, but she didn't finish that sentence.

"Every job matters. Can you afford to be turning someone down at this point?"

If she'd have been in front of me, I probably would have strangled her. My perfect younger sister, always the voice of reason and blah blah blah. "First of all, the guy was in the wrong, and he knows it. Second of all, you have no idea what it takes to run an event planning company, so don't talk like you do. I don't tell you how to teach your music classes, don't tell me how to run my business."

"I was just trying to help." Ava's voice had gone quiet.

"Well, don't."

I hung up on her. Honestly, I didn't know why I bothered. Why couldn't she have just listened, or tried to make me feel better? She was always so judgmental, so serious.

I chucked my phone on the passenger seat. I couldn't shake my inner rage, both at Tony, and now at Ava. I needed to relax. I needed to be zen. I couldn't understand how Ava was so calm and collected all the time. Probably because she'd never had real problems. Everything was easy for her.

Well, not for me. And nothing would calm me down except an afternoon at the spa.

"Juliet," I said over the phone. "I don't want any phone calls, voicemails, or emails. Nothing. Complete and utter silence, do you understand?"

"I understand," she replied, "but we've had a call from—"

"No calls!"

"But I don't know what to do about—"

"No work at all."

"And Mr. Reyes keeps—"

"COMPLETE AND UTTER SILENCE!" I screamed, and then hung up. I waited a minute, seeing if she would call back—in which case, FIRED! —but she didn't. Smart girl, that Juliet.

The rest of the day was a success. I was pampered, plucked, peeled, and exfoliated. I soaked in mud, drank only lemon water, and got a full-body massage by a man who looked like a Greek God. I left after shedding a layer of ickiness I didn't know was there, a whole new person.

And best of all, I didn't think of Tony Reyes once.

———

"We have a problem," was the first thing Juliet said to me the next morning when I entered the office.

I raised an eyebrow. She handed me my latte. I couldn't deal with problems until I had my latte.

I took a slow sip, warmth spreading all the way to my toes. I almost curled them, the latte was that good.

"Miss Elliot?"

I opened my eyes. I hadn't realized I'd closed them. "I'm not sure I want to start out my day with a problem, Juliet."

The corner of her eye twitched, but she said nothing. Juliet's name wasn't actually Juliet, it was Jules. When I interviewed her I made it very clear that I would never call her something so vulgar as *Jules*, and that if hired, she would be Juliet from then on. She never objected, although sometimes it caused random body parts to twitch, which I found somewhat amusing.

"I'm sorry, Miss Elliot, but this is urgent."

I sighed. "Oh fine." I walked into my office with Juliet trailing behind. It wasn't until I hung my coat and purse and was completely settled at my desk that I said, "Tell me this urgent problem?"

"The Higginbothams cancelled."

I sat up straighter. "What?"

"The Higgin—"

"Yes, I heard you. Why?"

"There was a sudden death in the family and now they need to plan a funeral instead of their party for International Goof Off Day."

"The nerve of them to cancel on us!"

"You thought the goof off party was ridiculous anyway," Juliet said.

"That's not the point! We had a contract. A binding, physical, sealed in blood…a contract."

"We get to keep the deposit, but otherwise, they're out free and clear."

My fingers tapped idly on the keyboard. "We'll just have to get another client." As peeved as I was that the Higginbothams had cancelled on me when I'd already started their portfolio, it wasn't a total loss.

"You'll have to cancel the venue," I said.

"Already done."

"And the flowers."

"Done."

"Did you call the caterer—"

"It's all been taken care of."

I shrugged. "Then we'll book someone new, now that we have time."

"That's not the problem."

I rolled my eyes. "Get to the point, Juliet."

"We needed that money. We have outstanding bills from the Freeman event that we can't pay back."

"What about the money from June's?"

"Already used up to pay for the Marcotti christening."

"But surely we made some profit. I mean, how do you think I pay for my spa days? And this new Lanvin purse?"

Juliet took a breath. "That's the point. You're spending more than you're making. Since you're not paying attention to the outstanding bills, you aren't getting the sense of what we owe."

My eyes narrowed. I wasn't an idiot, but Juliet was coming close to an accusation. "I take very great care to look at the profit margin from each event. I always make sure to budget, and not spend outside of that budget."

"But you're not taking taxes into account. Or the bills from this place. Only the event expenditures. We have more bills than that."

I crossed my arms over my chest. "Fine." Juliet was such a kill-joy. But I wasn't dumb enough that I wouldn't listen. I already knew what it was like to have to change your life when money went bye-bye. I wasn't going to put myself in that position and I wouldn't go asking Daddy for help. Oh, he'd help me, there was no question about that. But he was *proud* of me now. That was something I couldn't give up.

"I'll stop going to the spa." Every week. Maybe only every other week. Or once a month. If I could manage it.

"It still doesn't change the fact that we have outstanding bills that need to be paid ASAP. If we don't, we may end up losing the office."

Who says ASAP like it's a word? Juliet was getting on my nerves. "Then book me a new client. Surely there have been calls."

Juliet rubbed her fingers on her temples. "There have, but they've all been small...more intimate affairs."

"Meaning cheap."

"Meaning cheap," she echoed.

Ugh. People needed to get wise to the fact that to have a truly amazing party, one had to shell out. It was a truth universally acknowledged, or it should be.

"Stick to the phone like glue." I stood and gathered my things. "Let me know if you get anything worthwhile. I will have a chat with my father. He might know someone who needs our services." Dad had the best connections, and I could easily put the bug in his ear without telling him how desperately I needed a high-paying client.

Juliet followed me out of my office. "We may have to consider double-booking some of these smaller parties."

I spun around. "No. You know my feelings on that."

She ducked her head. "I know. But—"

"No buts. I'm not some cheap hire. I will only produce quality events. They have to be worth the time it takes me to do that. I'm building my brand here, and I don't want to deviate from it."

"Yes, Miss Elliot."

I shrugged on my coat. "I'll let you know if I come up with anything. You do the same."

She nodded. For a second, we both stared at the phone on her desk, willing it to ring. It didn't make a peep but I wanted to scream.

CHAPTER 4

DAD DIDN'T KNOW ANYONE WHO NEEDED A PARTY PLANNER RIGHT away, but he said he'd continue spreading the word about **Excessively Diverted**. Juliet hadn't received one promising phone call yet, so I told her to hit the streets, delivering my business card and pamphlet to companies that might need an event planner.

There was nothing for me to do but wait. Wait and eat.

The hostess led me to my table, and I nestled into the leather seat. "Sparkling water with lemon," I said when the waitress arrived. As much as I wanted, *needed*, a drink, I was on a budget here, and I'd have to forgo my Cabernet Sauvignon with lunch.

Someone pulled out the chair in front of me and I looked up. Tony Reyes sat, slinging his trench coat across his knees.

"What are you doing here?" I asked.

"I thought we could have lunch together."

I spluttered. "Why on earth would I want to do that?"

He played with the collar of his jacket. "We need to talk."

"I have nothing to say to you."

The waitress appeared, placing my water in front of me. "And what can I get you to drink?" she asked Tony.

"He's not staying."

"Coffee, please. Black."

She smiled at him. "I'll get that for you right away." Her hips swayed as she walked away. He didn't look.

"You're not staying," I said.

"Please, will you at least hear my apology?"

I crossed my arms over my chest. "What if I said no?"

"You'd have to personally remove me from this restaurant."

"I can scream you know. One shout of the word 'pervert' and you'd be gone in a snap."

He raised his hands. "Don't scream. I'm begging you."

Begging. I liked that. "I believe begging includes kneeling?"

His mouth tightened. "Miss Elliot—"

"Mr. Reyes."

"Why do you always—" He pinched the bridge of his nose and took a deep breath. "I'm sorry." He looked me in the eye. "For what I said and how I acted at June's party. I had a bad day and too much to drink, but that's not an excuse. I behaved poorly, toward you especially, and I am truly sorry."

I cocked my head. "Why are you bothering?"

His mouth opened in surprise.

"I suppose I should thank you for stalking me—"

"I didn't stalk you!"

"—just so you could come and apologize, but for some reason, I feel there's an ulterior motive here."

His face went still. I wanted to say "ha!" but I was a grown woman and would behave accordingly.

"Are you ready to order?" The waitress was back with Tony's coffee and a smile. For him, not me. I rolled my eyes. She had to be younger than me—though you could never be sure in LA—but Tony was old. Hair going gray old. But then, he oozed wealth from every orifice, and she was probably like my ex-friend Shelby: *Woman needing Botox seeking sugar daddy who will pay for multiple procedures. Age: inconsequential. The power to sign checks: a must.*

"We'll need another minute," Tony said and she left.

My eyes narrowed. "How did you know I was here?"

"I'm a powerful man."

"Or a stalker."

"I do not stalk—"

"Was that supposed to impress me, by the way? *I'm a powerful man.*" I imitated his deep voice.

"Do you talk to all of your clients this way?"

"Only the ones who annoy me. And you're not my client."

He glanced away. "Actually, that's why I'm here."

I grinned. "Now we get to it."

He leaned his elbows on the table, clasping his hands under his chin. "Miss Elliot, I would very much like to hire you to plan my daughter's Sweet Sixteen." His gaze was direct and piercing, as if he was trying to use mind-control. He was probably thinking, *don't drop eye contact and she'll agree.* It's what I would do.

"You mean, your daughter would very much like me to plan your daughter's Sweet Sixteen."

He blinked. "Yes."

"So you did all this stalking and apologizing because your daughter wants me as her party planner?"

His face turned red. The joy I felt over making him squirm was intense.

"I am a businessman. I recognize the quality in the product you offer, nothing more."

"And I recognize a load of crap in what you just said. The apology included."

"My apology was sincere and had nothing to do with my daughter wishing for you—" His mouth tightened. "I am truly ashamed at the way I behaved, and whether you accept my offer for hire or not, I will not withdraw my apology."

I crossed one leg over the other and studied him. Gray streaked his short black hair, he had a slight beard, and a pronounced crease between his dark eyebrows. His face was weathered, but handsome.

Way too old for my taste, though. I preferred my men young, hot, and a bit wild. Tony Reyes probably went to bed at nine, read the newspaper for fun, and had one of those containers that separated his daily vitamins.

Truth was, just the sight of him had my own body parts twitching, and not in a good way. But **Excessively Diverted** desperately needed the money. Lose my business, or suck it up and deal with this snobby douchebag? Sometimes I really hated being adult about things.

"What is your budget?" I asked. "How much are you willing to spend to make your daughter happy?"

"Anything."

He said it so easily, so matter-of-factly, I believed him. I almost liked him for it. Almost.

I pulled a notebook out of my purse, scrawled a number on it, tore out the page and gave it to him, being careful to keep my hands from shaking.

"This is the deposit I will require." I willed myself not to give my feelings away.

He glanced at the paper, then up at me. A strange expression crossed his face but I couldn't read it. "I will write you the check now."

My eyes widened and he noticed. I never did have much of a poker face. He handed me the check and I carefully tucked those precious zeroes into my wallet.

"Let's make an appointment for you to bring your daughter back to my office," I said.

"As soon as possible would be best," he replied.

"Can you tell me what your daughter is interested in? It will help me focus the portfolio I already made up."

The tone had shifted; it was all business between us now.

"She likes art, she paints. Modern over classical. She also dances ballet, she plays the flute, participates in various groups at school."

I took notes. "What is she like?"

He stared at my hand jotting down his words. "She's quiet, but she has a big group of friends. She's incredibly smart, but I think she hides it sometimes. She's strong, so very strong. I'm the only one who sees her vulnerability."

I met his eyes.

"That probably isn't what you meant."

"It was perfect." I hadn't expected that rawness and honesty about her. "I will have the portfolio ready by Friday. Are you able to come back then? Maybe over lunch or after your daughter finishes school?"

Tony pushed his chair back. "Friday is fine. Twelve thirty." He stood and held out his hand.

We shook, his skin hot against my skin. "Twelve thirty," I repeated.

CHAPTER 5

With the check Tony had given me, Juliet could stop her canvassing. The deposit was enough to pay all our outstanding bills from past events. I would never admit it out loud to Tony Reyes, but his daughter's party was a godsend.

"Hello, Miss Reyes, it's lovely to see you again." I motioned her to a chair across from my desk.

Tony's daughter looked at me askance, her eyes flicking to her father.

"And Mr. Reyes."

"Miss Elliot." He nodded at me. "Please, call me Antonio."

Doubtful. I may have been ready to suck it up and work with this guy for the money it would bring in, but I wasn't about to start calling him Antonio.

"Thank you for meeting with us." Mr. Reyes pulled the chair out for his daughter before taking his seat. "And this is Valentina."

"Vale," the girl said. "I prefer Vale."

I quickly sized her up. She was tall and slim, with full eyebrows and lips, and a sharp nose. Her hair was cut short, but it was chic. She wore a loose minidress and boots, an overabundance of jewelry,

22

her nails were gnawed on, but her makeup was done flawlessly. She was like a mix between Audrey Hepburn and J-Lo. Despite her age, she was already hovering between teenager and adult.

"Well Vale, Mr. Reyes, I've made up a portfolio of possible ideas for your Sweet Sixteen." I passed it over. "Of course, any of these can be tweaked, or if you would like to start completely from scratch, I can do that also."

They bent their heads over the portfolio. Silence filled the office except for the flipping of pages.

"These are all very lovely," Tony said, glancing up at me.

"Thank you." This polite stiffness was going to get old fast. After a few minutes I asked, "See anything you like, Vale?"

She was flipping between one page and another, her lip caught between her teeth.

"Anything can be changed to your wishes," I said. "If you had an idea, or color scheme, or specific theme, we can take that and go from there. I will give you ideas and input, but everything will be exactly the way *you* want it."

Tony watched her, waiting patiently. "What do you think, *mi vida*?"

"Yeah, I don't know…" She flipped back to the beginning. A matching crease to her father's appeared between her brows. Maybe she didn't like anything I'd put together.

"Can I ask you a question?" I said.

"Yes," Tony replied.

"I meant Vale."

She shrugged.

"Why me?" I leaned my elbows on my desk, curious for her answer. She went to a lot of trouble, or at least forced her father to go to a lot of trouble to hire me, but I had no clue why. I didn't know this girl. I doubt she'd been to one of my parties. How had she even heard of me?

She fidgeted. Her eyes flicked to her father and then back to the portfolio on her lap.

Tony's eyes met mine. I could tell by his face that he wanted the answer to this as much as I did.

"Vale," I said gently. Whatever the reason, she obviously didn't want to say. "I want to make sure you have the best Sweet Sixteen you can possibly imagine. Better, even. That's my goal with every client. So to start off, we need to get comfortable with each other. I want you to be able to tell me if something isn't exactly the way you want it, and I need to be comfortable telling you if something isn't going to work out."

She nodded. "I'm just, I'm not sure what I want."

"That's perfectly okay. Why don't we start with this. Email me things that you like. Pictures that make you feel something. Hobbies that you have, movies or books that you're into. Music. Anything and everything. If it inspires you, or makes you smile, or lifts you in some way, email it to me. That way I can get to know you a bit better, and that will give me a starting point."

"Okay."

"Okay." I handed her my card. "My email address is on here, plus my cell. You can contact me anytime." My gaze moved to Tony. "Do you have a date set, so I have some idea of time frame?"

"Nothing concrete," he replied, "but her birthday is in two months."

"Excellent. Not a lot of time for venue, but everything else is completely doable."

"It will be at our house. Right, *mi vida*?"

"Sure, whatever."

It was a flippant response, but I could tell she really didn't mind. Or maybe she was too preoccupied between two different sheets in the portfolio. She kept flipping between them.

"Well, that makes things easier." I avoided looking at Tony. "I'll have to stop by sometime, to get an idea of layout."

"Of course."

"Do you like those two?" I asked Vale.

She bit her lip. "I do. Sort of."

Sort of. I could work with sort of.

"All right. I'll keep those in mind, but start sending me pictures right away. The sooner we have a theme, the better."

Tony stood, and Vale followed suit. She handed me the portfolio.

"Take it with you," I said. "In case something in there grows on you."

"My mom," she blurted, hugging the portfolio to her chest. Tony froze. "She was at your *Pillow Talk* party."

Tony's jaw had gone rigid. I had no idea who his wife was, but the mere mention of her had turned him to frost.

"Oh," I said, at a complete loss for something more sensible. "Well... I'm glad she had a good time."

"Come, Valentina," Tony said.

She gave me an apologetic shrug before following her father from my office. Whatever that was about, hopefully it wouldn't get in the way of the biggest client I had ever landed.

CHAPTER 6

AT HOME, I FOUND MY DAD PUFFING AWAY ON THE TREADMILL. HE was jogging at an incline, his face beet red and sweat pooling under his armpits.

"Dad! You're going to give yourself a heart attack!"

He slowed the treadmill to a walk. "Nonsense. I need to get into shape."

"You are in shape." I opened a window to let in some fresh air.

"Better shape. I'm doing a new ad for Botticelli For Men."

"You are? That's great!" Dad's first ad with BFM was for their new line of face creams. He'd looked so handsome in his dark suit, staring off into the distance while clutching the jar of cream in one hand.

"What about you? Have you found a new client? I've asked around but all of my friends are boring lately."

I turned the TV off, then settled onto the stationary bike beside Dad. "I do have a new client. A high paying client."

"I knew you could do it!" Dad puffed. His hands gripped the bars. "Who is it?"

"His name is Antonio Reyes. It's a Sweet Sixteen for his daughter."

"Never heard of him. What does he do?"

I shrugged. "CEO of something." Juliet had told me all about his company and what he did but my mind had wandered after two words. "He's loaded. No expenses spared for this thing, and he already wrote me a down payment check." Which was long gone. What a disappointment. I could've bought a new handbag, but noooo, I had to be all adult about things now.

Dad turned off the treadmill. He wiped a towel across his brow. "Is he young? Handsome? Wrinkle-free?"

"No, yes, and no. He's old—" Tony Reyes was younger than Dad so I had to watch my mouth. "I mean, he's in his forties probably. But he's definitely not wrinkle-free. He wears his age, unlike you."

Dad slumped into a chair. My father usually looked pretty amazing, but right then he appeared haggard and pale. It was probably the exercise. Whoever said it took years off your age was a fool.

"But he's handsome?" Dad pressed.

"He has a certain something." It was probably just the money. The right suit, haircut and accessories could make almost any man attractive.

"Handsome or not, I'm glad you have a client after that other person backed out on you. I've already blacklisted them amongst my friends and acquaintances."

"Thanks, Dad, you're the best." I went to kiss him on the cheek, then thought better of it. I loved my father, but I did not love sweat.

"I need to shower," he said, reading my mind. "Let me know how it goes."

"You too. I want to hear all about your new ad campaign."

He slung the towel over his neck. "Dinner tonight?"

"I'll schedule you in."

I followed the directions on my car's NAV to the Reyes house. It was nestled in a gated community in Brentwood. The driveway was a steep incline then suddenly, the house came into view—a two-story Spanish-style mansion with pale stucco and those wavy roof tiles. It reminded me of my sister Ava's house that she and her new husband had bought after they married. I disliked it right away.

A maid let me in, and I waited inside the foyer, the window above shining a beam of sunlight right on top of my head. The sun was hot and I thought of moving, but then figured I might look a bit angelic and decided to stay put.

Vale appeared from an arched doorway, her fingers moving furiously over her cellphone. She was wearing leggings and a belted sweater. "Sorry, my dad isn't here yet."

"Oh?" I asked as she led me into a living room. So much for my angelic moment. Tony wasn't here and Vale hadn't even glanced up from her phone.

"He's at work. He's maybe on his way. Don't know how long it will take."

I sat down. "We can talk ideas while we're waiting. Or you can give me the tour yourself?"

It took her a couple of minutes to finish whatever she was doing and put the phone down. "Dad will show you around. He's weird about strangers in the house."

I frowned. This coming from the man who was throwing a party here. Maybe he had a crazy wife up in his attic. I listened for banging noises or shrieking but heard nothing.

"Then let's talk ideas," I said. "I received your email yesterday. Lots of excellent stuff in there, we just need to narrow down our focus."

Vale chewed a nail. She would barely look at me. "Okay."

Was she into this or not? She'd gone to a lot of trouble to hire me, and now she seemed completely uninterested.

"Or, I can hash it all out with your father, if you'd prefer."

She dropped her hand. Her eyes flashed at me. "No. No way. I get to do this."

"Okay."

"Okay."

Silence. She stared at me. I stared back. She said nothing. I tried not to tear my own hair out. Were all teenagers like this?

Her shoulders slumped, she dropped her gaze. "I had a quinceañera last year. The woman my dad hired wouldn't let me choose anything. It was all about what she wanted, and my dad just let her. This time, I get to choose."

Then choose, I wanted to shout. But I kept my cool. "I'm all ears."

She gave me one of those teenager looks like she had no clue what I was talking about and didn't care.

"I am here for you and what you want," I said, for probably the billionth time.

She picked at her cuticle. She mumbled something.

"I'm sorry, what?"

"I don't know what I want. I just know I want it to be what *I* want."

I was never having kids. Ever.

I pulled out the prints she'd emailed and laid them on the coffee table in front of me. "Let's start here. In looking at all of these, I see some similarities. A lot of dark colors, but nothing stark or sombre. It's all very pretty."

Vale made a face.

"Not frou-frou pretty. Glamorous, without being glitzy or over-the-top."

She nodded. We were getting somewhere.

"Some of it is very old-world. Vintage, or...that's not the right word. Historical? Am I right?"

She bit her lip. "I guess."

"A few things come to mind right off the top of my head. How about a masquerade?"

"Overdone."

"Okay. Romeo and Juliet?"

"They die at the end. Not very festive."

"Right. We could go the fairy tale route. Fairy tales in general or do one in particular?"

"Too Disney."

She was a tough one. "Understood." I glanced through the pictures. One was of a famous painting—I wouldn't have recognized it if it weren't for my dad. Tony had said something about Vale being into art. I pulled the picture closer and examined it. "This is a Botticelli, yes?"

She nodded.

Three of the four people in the painting were naked. Couldn't go there for a Sweet Sixteen. There were flowers...too old lady. And wings...but fallen angels were overdone as well. I backed away from the picture, trying to get a broader view. Vale was quiet. When I glanced up, she was staring at me.

"Why this?" I asked.

She shrugged. "I like it."

"Do you paint?" I wasn't going to admit her father had already told me stuff about her. If there was one thing I remembered about being a teenager, it was that privacy was number one.

"Yeah. I mean, I try. I like art. Renaissance art especially."

Brain click. "What about the Renaissance for a theme?"

She blinked.

"From the little I've seen of the house, it would fit in well." A lot easier than if she wanted something like Under the Sea, or Alice in Wonderland. "We could have paintings brought in, drape some of the walls with heavy cloth. Your dress could be very Elizabeth the first."

Vale didn't respond, but her eyes had brightened. That was a good sign.

"I would have to do some research. I honestly don't know much about it, but I'm sure we could make your house look like a castle, or cathedral. We could have a throne for you to sit on, and you could receive your guests as they come in. Or we could have it outside, use tents and lots of florals, twisting vines, candles. Maybe go more modern renaissance?"

"I—" Vale was interrupted by the arrival of her father.

It was about time.

CHAPTER 7

"I'M SO SORRY I'M LATE." HE KISSED VALE ON THE CHEEK, THEN looked at me. I raised an eyebrow. No way was he kissing me anywhere.

"It's okay, Dad," Vale replied, but her face said otherwise.

No way was I going to let him get away with being late, either.

"Actually, it's not okay." I crossed my legs. "We had an appointment. For one o'clock. It is now one-thirty-nine."

He scowled. "I know. And I apologized for it."

I stood up. "Are you usually late for meetings?"

"No, I—"

"So it's just me then. You don't respect my time."

"Of—"

"Or is this a sexist thing? I'm a woman, I've got all the time in the world... I was probably late, too, because women are never ready on time?"

"Miss Elliot—"

"This was a business appointment, which you agreed to. If you couldn't make it, you should have called." There was something about this guy that put me in fighting mode. I knew I should've been more professional, but I couldn't let him win.

He rubbed his hand over his forehead. Vale was watching with her mouth slightly open. "I did make it. I'm here."

"Well, we talked without you." I slung my purse over my shoulder. "I now have to be going. I'm sure your daughter can fill you in on what you missed. If not, let's set up another appointment. But maybe for thirty-nine minutes later than you think you can make it, just in case."

With my chin high, I stalked from the room. I knew Tony Reyes' type, I'd known them all my life. The kind who thought they were the most important being in the world. No one mattered as much as them. Everyone else would adhere to their schedule, their way, their wants. I knew that type because secretly, I was that type myself sometimes. But I liked it a lot better *being* that person rather than the one who was left in their wake.

"Miss Elliot."

His footsteps echoed behind me but I ignored them.

"Miss Elliot, stop." A hand grabbed my elbow before I could reach the front door. I turned to face him. His gaze found mine and didn't let go.

"I am sorry. The meeting I was in ran over, and then there was an accident on the highway. However, I should have called, like you said."

He actually looked repentant. But I wasn't going to give in so easily. "Yes, you should have."

"Next time, I will."

"Next time?" My voice rose. *"Next time?"*

"If there is a next time."

"There won't be a next time." I pulled my elbow from his grip. "You may not value my time, but I do."

"I do—"

"And there isn't only me to consider. You told me you would do anything for your daughter, and for this party. Anything should include being here when you say you will. She might let you get away with it, but I won't."

"I can see that," he said wryly. His lips twitched like he was laughing at me.

My eyes narrowed. "Good bye."

"Wait, please." He reached for me again then must've thought better of it because he dropped his hand. "At least let me show you around the house. That way you don't have to come back again so soon."

Point taken.

"Fine."

"Excellent."

Oh, his fake smile was good. "I really dislike you." I hadn't meant to say that out loud.

He laughed. "That hurts. Truly." He motioned for me to follow. "We'll start with the kitchen."

"I've disliked a lot of people in my time, believe me. In fact, I dislike most everyone. But you're nearing the top of the list."

He turned to face me, pushing the door behind him open with his back. "What happens when I become number one?"

My smile was not fake, it was real, and it was evil. "You'll have to wait and see."

He paused, staring at me, an unreadable expression on his face. "You know, I'm almost looking forward to it."

CHAPTER 8

I STARTED COLLECTING IDEAS ON MODERN RENAISSANCE. I researched online, made a Pinterest board, and even went to a museum for a private tour on renaissance artists. Some of what I found was super cheesy—cakes with swords sticking out of them, cheap looking costumes, tacky party games. But I found some real beauty amidst the tacky.

I met Vale again on Saturday for lunch. Her father wasn't invited.

"Have you looked at my Pinterest board?" I asked. I'd emailed her the link earlier in the week.

"Yeah. I liked a lot of it." She sipped her soda.

"But?" It was unspoken, but I heard it.

"It's hard to see how it will look. One party. One place. How it all goes together, know what I mean?"

"I know exactly what you mean." Vale was still shy with me, but she was gradually opening up. "That's what I'm here for, though. To make sense of the madness."

She almost smiled. The waiter brought our food—a salad for me and pasta for her. We ate in silence for a few minutes.

"I…" Vale was stirring her noodles around her plate. "I did

35

something with one of the centerpieces. I mean, I copied the pictured you pinned, then changed it a bit. As a drawing."

My eyebrows rose. "Can I see it?"

She ducked her head. "Sure. If you want."

"Definitely."

She pulled a sketchbook out of her purse. Under the table, my foot twitched. If her drawing was horrible, I'd have to lie and say I liked it, then try and steer her in another direction.

Vale handed it to me, the book open to a sketch done in pencil. It was of a tall metal centerpiece, the shape unknown because flowers wrapped around it in a full twist. Bunches of grapes and greenery intermixed with the flowers. Tapered candles wreathed the very top.

I gasped. It wasn't even fake. "This is gorgeous. What did the original look like?"

Vale's face flushed. "Flip back a page."

The original was a small vase of flowers with one candle sticking out of the top. Vale's design was one hundred times better.

"I love this."

She wouldn't meet my eyes. "Really?"

"Yes! You are very talented."

She shoved a bite of pasta in her mouth.

"Can I look through the whole thing?"

Her shoulders went to her ears. "I guess. I mean…some of it isn't very good. It's just a sketchbook."

I went back to the beginning and flipped through the pages, marvelling at the work of an almost sixteen-year-old. Most of it was done in pencil, and she did it all well, at least to my untrained eye. She'd drawn makeup ideas and outfits, lavish houses, portraits. She'd recreated famous paintings, and there was a pretty good self-portrait.

"Have you thought of your dress?" I asked, examining some of the gowns she'd drawn. I wasn't sure if they were her designs or copies, but they all looked fab.

She shrugged. I would've bet my Birkin, she had.

"I know a few designers. If you want to sketch your dress, I'm sure we could have it made. It would be one of a kind."

Vale started to grin, but bit her lip to stop it. Either she was still uncomfortable around me, which I understood since we didn't know each other that well, or she just didn't know how to be happy.

"Think about it, anyway." I stopped on a portrait she'd done of her father. At least, I thought it was Tony Reyes. But she'd made him look different... Younger, maybe? More handsome, definitely, but I couldn't tell exactly how. With narrowed eyes, I tilted the picture, trying to figure it out.

"What are you looking at?" Vale asked.

I showed her, smiling so she wouldn't think I was judging her work.

"Oh. Dad."

Exactly. Oh, him. I handed it to her. She brushed a finger over the paper. "This is one of my favorites."

I couldn't imagine why.

She turned back to a sketch of a woman I'd passed without really noticing.

"My mom."

I took a sip of my sparkling water. "May I?"

She turned it toward me. The woman was beautiful, with thick dark hair and full lips. Vale had drawn her gaze slightly to the left, like she was looking past you. She wasn't smiling.

"Is this recent?" I asked, not sure what to say. This was the second time Vale had brought her up, but when Tony had been around, he hadn't been keen to talk about her.

"About six months ago," Vale said quietly. "I haven't seen her since."

Uncomfortable, my gaze darted around. What was I supposed to say to that? I wasn't a therapist, or her guidance counselor.

"Your parents are divorced?"

She nodded. "I talk to her, and stuff, I just don't see her anymore. She moved to Manhattan."

"She doesn't visit?"

Vale shrugged.

"She should visit." Vale glanced at me, and I dropped my gaze. I wasn't sure where that came from, but I believed it. My mother wouldn't have done that to me, to us. Neither would Dad. Not that I was the foremost authority on motherhood, but ignoring your own child was the height of selfishness. Not that I was the authority on unselfishness, either.

Vale was stirring her pasta around again. "Dad won't talk about her."

"I noticed." A thought occurred to me. Maybe she wanted her mother at the party, but Tony wouldn't allow it. I suppressed a groan. Getting caught in the middle of family drama was way above my paygrade.

Okay, maybe not above this paygrade, but I still didn't want to get involved.

"So you like my centerpiece?" Vale asked, and I was relieved at the change in subject.

"I do."

"I was thinking, this could be on round tables. But my table would be long, kinda like a wedding?" Vale was talking fast now. "Like, the head table? And instead of this, I could have something... I have an idea but I haven't drawn it yet. Can I show it to you when I do?"

"Let's plan to meet up in a week. Sketch that idea, and meanwhile, I'll get moving on the tent, the tables and chairs, and the lights. Sound good?"

We'd decided to hold the party outside. It was southern California, we might as well make use of the beautiful weather. Besides, you could do more outside, and this way we wouldn't have so many strangers inside Tony's house, creeping him out or whatever.

"Sounds good," Vale replied.

It was more than good. This party would be, in the words of Valentina Reyes, totally epic.

CHAPTER 9

"WHO IS THAT WOMAN AND WHAT IS SHE DOING?"

I rolled my eyes. Men had no business butting into the party planning. Not even the men with the platinum credit card.

Tony Reyes watched Juliet scramble on her knees in the grass, stretching out a measuring tape along the lawn. Good thing she was wearing a skirt, otherwise—grass stains. Although she was *this close* to a wardrobe malfunction.

I had my notebook out and was jotting down numbers. Tony motioned at Juliet. "Is she a professional?"

"She's taking measurements." Obviously.

"There's an easier way. I can get you the lot blue prints."

"I like to be exact." Besides, Juliet needed something to do.

Tony frowned. "Human error. She's using a measuring tape."

"Who do you think makes up the blue prints in the first place?" Not that I had any clue. Didn't want him to know that though. "You still haven't emailed me the guest list. I need it right away."

"I'm working on it."

"Not fast enough."

His jaw clenched.

"It's not hard. Just sit down and make the list. I can't order tables, chairs, place settings, anything, until I know the kind of numbers I'll be working with."

"Fine."

I smiled sweetly. "I'll thank you when I get it."

Tony continued to watch Juliet. "Speaking of… Thank you for holding the party outside."

I snorted. "Please."

"I know you didn't do it for me," he said, "but thank you all the same."

I glanced at him. He wasn't smirking or sneering or smiling or anything that meant sarcasm. He actually meant it.

"I'll still need to stage it from inside. The caterer will have to use your kitchen."

He took a breath. "The fewer people inside the house, the better."

"I'll keep that in mind."

Vale came outside then. She had her sketchbook tucked under one arm. "Hi, Beth!" she said, giving me a big smile.

I blinked. "Hi…"

She hesitated. "Oh. Sorry. Am I not supposed to call you… should I say Ms. Elliot?"

"No, of course not. Beth is fine." I didn't ask her why she was in such a good mood. Probably not a good question for a teenager. I motioned to her sketchbook. "Do you have new pictures to show me?"

"Yeah, I've been working on my dress. I keep changing my mind, or it doesn't turn out like I want it to, but I kinda like this one." She handed me the book, open to a page. "What do you think?"

The dress had long sleeves and a low, square neckline. The skirt flowed out from the waist and beadwork covered the fitted bodice and trailed down the skirt.

"It's gorgeous! What color are you thinking?"

"I don't know…"

Tony leaned over my shoulder to see the sketch. I angled it away.

I studied Vale's coloring. Dark hair and olive skin—she could pull off anything. "Deep red is my first thought, so maybe that's too obvious. What's your favorite color?"

"Don't say black," Tony said.

"Dad."

"Oh, you can't wear black," I said. "You'll look like you're in mourning."

She swore under her breath.

"Valentina!" her father barked. She rolled her eyes.

"If you're set on this, we can take it in. I have a designer in mind. She'll be able to show you some fabrics and you can decide the color then."

She took the sketchbook back. "I might want to tweak it some more."

"Sure. Just let me know when you're ready. Meanwhile." I put my hands on my hips and glared at Tony. "Get on your father about the guest list."

"Whatever," she mumbled, walking away.

Juliet walked over, brushing grass off her knees. I handed her my notebook so she could jot down her measurements.

"I'm Antonio," Tony said, holding his hand out to Juliet.

"And she's busy," I snapped. "So are you. You have things to do. Like the guest list. And your own costume. Have you decided what you're going to wear?"

His eyebrows hiked up to his hairline. "Costume?"

He looked slightly afraid. It was awesome. "Yes, costume. I'm sure Vale told you the theme: Modern Renaissance."

"Then I'll go modern and wear a suit."

"You will not. If you're going to be at this party, you have to dress appropriately."

"Since when is a suit not appropriate?"

"Since I said so."

He crossed his arms over his chest. "I am a grown man. I do not wear costumes."

"You do now."

"No."

"Are you going to stomp your feet next? Maybe throw a tantrum?"

His face reddened. "You—"

I leaned toward him. "Anything for your daughter."

The fight went out of him. "I wish I'd never said that out loud," he grumbled.

"I'll let Vale know."

"Do you ever lose a fight?"

"Who said this is a fight? This is me, telling you what to do." I held up a finger. Then another. "Guest list. Costume. If I don't get that list, prices will go up for late orders. And if you don't order your own costume, I'll do it for you." Now that would be fun. I was already thinking mustard yellow tights and a doublet. Maybe a hat with a feather sticking out of it.

"You're worse than my ex-wife."

"Why, because I'm not going anywhere?"

His whole face hardened.

I'd hit below the belt. For some reason, I felt bad about it.

That was new.

CHAPTER 10

THE PHONE HADN'T STOPPED RINGING SINCE I CAME INTO THE OFFICE. If it wasn't for Juliet, I probably would've stabbed my own eyes out. She really did deserve something, like a raise, or a bonus, or a five-dollar Starbucks gift card.

"The guy from the lighting store called," she said, "and he won't rent out their chandeliers, no matter what you offer. It's against their policy."

I cursed. I wanted those chandeliers—they were the best I'd found online. "We'll have to try wedding supply instead," I said. "I'll look into it."

A minute later. "The caterer doesn't want to do the fruit tarts for dessert. She wants to make a dome cake filled with chocolate and nut cream. Is that okay?"

"I'll have to check with the clients first."

I had just enough time to take a sip of my latte before, "That dinnerware you found on Etsy? They said they can make two hundred within the time-frame, but no more than that."

"Tell them to start anyway. I don't want to end up with less."

I called Tony Reyes about fifty different names in my head.

Then I called him on the phone. "I need that guest list now," I griped.

He sighed. "Hello, Ms. Elliot."

"You don't have time for hellos. Get me what I need."

"Isn't the general count enough for you?"

"No. Two hundred can become three hundred, then four, then five. I've seen it happen. I can't make definitive orders on anything until I have that number."

"I promise you it will be no more than two hundred. Does that satisfy you?"

"I'll only be satisfied once I have the guest list in hand."

"I didn't realize you were such an easy woman to please."

I grumbled. "Do you want no one to show up to this party?"

He didn't answer.

"Never mind. I'm calling Vale." We texted every day now, mostly about the party, but she had started to open up to me in a way I hadn't expected. Random stuff mostly, about what a teacher said in school, or what nasty thing some boy had done, or about a pair of shoes her friend had that she wanted. I was wary about getting too personal. Vale seemed to like talking to me, probably because she had no mother-figure in her life, but what would happen once the party was over?

"Bringing out the big guns, I see," Tony said.

"If she's the only one you'll listen to."

"Not the only one."

Oh, how I hated him. "If you're not going to respect me, then I quit right now."

He groaned. "Always the drama queen."

"Don't talk like you know me," I snapped.

"Don't give me ultimatums. I've paid you to do a job. Now do it."

I almost screamed. Instead, I took a few calming breaths. I was impressed by my own maturity. "Do you not understand how a party works?" I asked slowly, as if talking to a toddler. "You invite people, and they come. But I cannot invite people, when I don't know who these people are. Hence, no one comes." I was proud of myself. Not only had I kept calm, I'd also said hence. "If I don't know how many are coming, there won't be enough food, enough chairs, enough tables, enough party favors, enough—"

"I get it."

Oh no, he did not get to interrupt me. "Then get me that list." I hung up and texted Vale.

Me: Your father still won't give me the guest list. I need it ASAP. Can you get on him?
Vale: I have.
Vale: It's complicated.

I rubbed my temples.

Me: Is there some way I can help?

Not that I wanted to help *him*.

Vale: He has the list. But there's one problem.

I waited.

Vale: It's my mom. I want her to come. He doesn't. It's been a big fight. I won't let him give it to you until her name is on it.

Oh brother.

Me: She's your mother, of course she should be invited.
Vale: He hates her.
Vale: And her boyfriend.
Vale: I don't want her bf there either. He's like, 20. But I want her there.

I'd rather wear thrift store clothes than get in the middle of this.

Me: Do you want me to talk to him for you?
Vale: Would you?

Tony said he'd do anything for Vale, and I was starting to realize why. It was like she had this strange power to make people like her. I hated kids. I should say no.

Me: Yes.

I cursed Tony Reyes. It was becoming more and more clear that every problem surrounding this party was his fault. It was nice having someone to blame.

"It's me again," I said into my cellphone.

He sighed. Loudly. "I'm busy."

This wasn't getting off to a good start. "I talked to Vale."

"Of course you did."

"Of course I did. This is her party."

"Did you have a point? Or were you rubbing it in my face that you speak with my daughter more than I do these days."

I paused, my mouth open. But I was never good at tact. Might as well just plow ahead. "This is about her mother. The guest list I mean."

He was quiet.

"Look, I understand if you don't want your ex there."

"Do you?" His voice sounded dangerously calm.

"Yes, I do. But this isn't about your ex. It's about Vale's mom."

"That is exactly my problem," he replied.

I frowned. "What do you mean?"

"Nita treated me like dirt. She cheated, ran off with a twenty-two-year-old *manscaper*, and took half my money with her. But that's not why I don't want her here."

I was still, as if one movement would make him stop talking, not that he could see me.

"She is a horrible example to our daughter. She thinks what she did was funny. Like a cute little anecdote to tell at parties, never mind the pain she caused. Never mind that she has a fifteen-year-old who sees everything. Who spent her childhood being ignored, but suddenly she has become Nita's best friend. Not because Nita sees the value and goodness in her own child, or how talented and smart she is, but because she wants to get back at me. Nita has never cared about Valentina. Never. Valentina grew up with different nannies while Nita spent her days making friends with Chianti. Valentina misses her mother, of course she does. But I would rather Valentina miss the idea of a mother, rather than the reality of a woman who never deserved the honor."

I swallowed. "I'm sorry. I didn't realize—"

"Of course you didn't. I don't splash around my family issues for all to see. But can you understand now the position I'm in?"

I did. He didn't want to disappoint his daughter, but he didn't want that woman anywhere near her. "Do you think she'd actually come? Vale said she lives in Manhattan now."

His voice took on a tone of resignation. "Part of me thinks she wouldn't bother with the time or expense. She didn't come to Valentina's quinceañera, but her interest in our daughter started afterward. She has been trying hard lately to be in contact with Valentina. The things she says to her, the lies and manipulation… Valentina tells me everything. She still trusts me. But Nita is doing her best to change that. I wouldn't put it past her to come, just for that reason."

This was way out of my depth. I couldn't tell Antonio what to do. I had experience with unruly party guests or requests to keep so-and-so away from so-and-so, but this was more than that. This was a complicated family affair that no well-timed diversion or refereeing could fix.

"Have you spoken to Vale about why you're reluctant to have her mother at the party?"

"No. Despite my issues with Nita, I don't want to speak badly about her to Valentina."

I sighed. "I'm sorry." I couldn't believe I'd just said that out loud to Tony Reyes. "I can't tell you what to do in this situation.

And I'm sorry I'm going to have to ask again, but I do need that guest list. Is it possible to give it to me without her name on it, and then I can add one...or two, if you decide to extend an invitation?"

"It's not that simple, or I already would have done so. There are people who would refuse to come if they knew she'd be there. Nita burned many bridges before she left."

An idea began to form in my mind, but if Antonio knew, he probably wouldn't go along with it. "Put her on the guest list."

"Excuse me?"

He was angry. I ignored it. "I will take care of it. She won't be there. But put her on the guest list so Vale can see."

"I don't understand."

"You don't have to understand, you just have to trust me."

"But I don't trust you."

"I guess it's time to start."

CHAPTER 11

I received the guest list a half an hour later by email. At the bottom, Nita Oliver plus guest. Antonio Reyes trusted me.

The solution was easy. I would send Nita Oliver an invitation, but I would misspell the address. One number off the zip code and it would never reach its destination. The kind of mistake anyone could make. If Vale or Antonio (or Nita) found out, I would apologize, but the party would be over and it would be too late by then.

My phone beeped with another text as I was ordering the invitations. *Antonio again?* I thought, my heart rate increasing.

Vale: Can you come over?
Me: What's up?
Vale: I need help with something.
Vale: Please?

I looked at my extensive to-do list and sighed.

Me: Be there in 20.

Vale was puffy-eyed and red-cheeked when I arrived.

"What's wrong?" I asked, as she pulled me upstairs into her room. I'd never been inside before, Antonio hadn't shown me the bedrooms when he gave me the tour.

It was a riot of colors and clothes, bed unmade and shoes spilling out of her open closet. She'd painted random things on one wall—flowers and trees, dresses and faces, butterflies and swirls. Postcards of famous art covered another wall. My room as a teenager had posters of models and actors. Such a cliché.

"Vale, what's going on?" I asked as she gathered clothes into her arms and shoved them into her closet, which was almost the size of another bedroom.

"Sorry. My mom isn't answering, and I didn't know who else to call, and you know all about parties so I thought…"

Confusion lowered my brow. Was this about the party, or her mom, or what?

She let go of the clothes in her arms and they tumbled to the floor. I waited, still standing awkwardly in the doorframe.

"Never mind. It's stupid."

I almost rolled my eyes. I'd come all the way over here and she was pulling this? "I'm sure it's not stupid."

She bit her lip.

I sat on the edge of her bed and then patted the spot beside me. It's what my mom would've done. Except she would've wrapped her arms around me like I was the most important person right then.

Vale sat. I didn't hug her.

"Tell me what's wrong."

"It's just… there's this girl at school. She's sort of a friend, sort of not."

"Like a frenemy?" I asked.

Vale made a face. "I guess. Anyway, she already had her Sweet Sixteen and she thinks it was the best thing ever. It *was* a pretty great party, they even filmed it for some reality show." Vale picked at her black nail polish. "So she's been making all these comments like mine won't be as good, you know? Like she has any clue because I've barely told her anything, but still."

Sounded about right. Teenage girls never changed. The drama, the backbiting. Vale probably thought this was the worst thing in the world to happen to her.

"Anyway, now she's asking who my date is. Every class I see her, she's all, 'has someone asked you yet? Do you have a date yet?' I didn't know I was supposed to have a date. Am I supposed to have a date?"

"It's your party, you can do what you want."

"I know but..."

Clearly she didn't subscribe to the Elizabeth Elliot way of thinking: never let anyone push you around, or tell you what to do. "Tell her you'd rather flirt with all the boys, instead of being stuck with only one."

"She'll think that's an excuse."

True.

"Am I really supposed to have a date? It seems weird for someone to ask me to my own party. But I don't want to ask anyone either."

"Are your other friends bringing dates?"

She shook her head. "Well, Sonja has a boyfriend so he's coming, but the rest of them aren't."

"Then why should you? Unless you want to. But there's no rule saying the birthday girl has to have a date at her Sweet Sixteen."

"It's not one of those unspoken things that everybody just knows?"

"No."

She let out a breath.

"Do you want me to uninvite her?"

She hesitated. "I shouldn't. It'll just make things worse at school."

"I'll punch her in the mouth for you. I'm not above it. I can get scrappy."

Vale laughed, her whole demeanor relaxed. "I'll keep that in mind. But don't tell Dad, he wouldn't like it."

"Don't tell me what?"

My head whipped toward the door. Antonio was leaning against the frame, his arms folded, his lips curved up in a smile.

"Oh, nothing," I said. "Secrets between girls."

"Then I won't ask." One corner of his mouth lifted. "I wouldn't want you to get scrappy on me."

For the love.

"Dad! How long were you standing there?"

"Long enough to know that if you need a date, I'm available."

Vale buried her face in her hands and groaned.

I rose from the bed, shooting him a look of disgust. "Don't be such an old man."

His eyes swept over me. Suddenly, he didn't seem so old.

"Are you hip on the teenagers now?" he asked as I walked toward him.

"Hip enough to know that 'hip' isn't a hip word anymore."

"*Ohmygosh,*" Vale said behind me.

Antonio looked like he was about to laugh. I narrowed my eyes at him before turning back to Vale.

"Are you all good now? Offer still stands." I fisted my hand in front of my chest where Antonio wouldn't see.

Vale snorted. "I'm fine," she said.

"Seriously, though, it's *your* party. *You* get to decide what you want and what you don't want. Believe that, and when you tell this girl, she'll believe it too."

She looked thoughtful. "Thanks, Beth."

I nodded. Turning back around, I caught Antonio's stare. There was something in his expression that I couldn't read. He followed me out of the room and down the stairs.

"Valentina called you?" he asked when we reached the front door.

"She said she needed help."

"And you came."

I didn't tell him I'd thought it was a party problem. Which it sort of was.

"Do you do this for all your clients?"

I hadn't realized how close he was, the tips of his shoes hitting the tips of mine. His tie was loose, the open collar of his shirt drawing my eyes to his neck.

"My clients don't usually call me for friendship advice." When I glanced back up, he was looking at my lips. I swallowed.

"Is that what it was?"

"I don't know. I'm not good at advice in general." Why had I admitted that out loud? Just because he'd opened up to me about his ex-wife, didn't mean I needed to get all personal with him.

"You did just fine."

I took a step back, this sudden change in our relationship throwing me.

"Thank you, Elizabeth." The way he said it—sincere and heart-felt—I didn't know how to respond. It was much easier to bicker and banter with him than do this.

I pulled on the bottom of my blazer, lifted my chin, and said, "You're welcome." Like a professional, and hopefully not like someone who valued those words more than she would ever admit.

CHAPTER 12

I NEEDED A BREAK. NEEDED TO IGNORE MY RESPONSIBILITIES, MY WORK, my assistant who kept calling, that weird interaction with Tony. So I decided to go to a party I hadn't put any work into. Dad invited me to a charity function benefiting some hospital or school or poor people or something. I put on a new dress and went along.

"What do you think?" Dad asked as we walked inside.

The lights were too bright, the decorations cheap, and a slideshow was playing some sort of tacky video on repeat. "They should've hired me to plan this thing."

Dad patted my hand over his arm. "That they should have."

We worked the room, Dad with his killer looks and charm, and me and my killer looks and...who was I kidding? My killer looks were enough. The room was full of handsome men in suits who smelled like cologne and money. I smiled and flirted. I sipped champagne and tossed my hair. But I was bored. I had no idea why—I usually loved these things. Bad decorating was probably to blame.

"Beth?"

I turned at the sound of my name and there was Vale wearing a ballerina style dress, her short hair curled to beachy waves. Dad continued his lap of the room without me.

"What are you doing here?" I asked as she threw her arms around me. Her hugs were becoming the norm, I didn't even want to push her away anymore.

She pulled back. "I came with my dad. He sorta made me."

I scanned the room but didn't see Tony. "Are you having fun?"

She rolled her eyes.

"Yeah, me neither." I linked my arm with hers and spoke low. "I mean, have you seen the décor? They're two balloon animals away from a circus."

Vale giggled. It reminded me she was just a kid. She often seemed more grown-up than her fifteen years. Most of the time now it was like we were...friends.

"What about the food," she said. "Those weird sushi-thingies they have going on?"

I made a face at her and we both laughed.

"Did you talk to that girl at school?" I asked.

"Yeah." She fiddled with the ends of her hair. "I did what you said, and she stopped bugging me about it."

"That's good, right?"

"I dunno. I think she's saying stuff behind my back now." She shrugged. "But at least she's too scared to say it to my face. That's something."

Thatta girl. I tightened my arm on hers. "I sent the invitations this morning, but I can try to get hers back."

"I thought you were going to offer to punch her again."

"Or that."

Vale smiled. "Dad."

I looked up. Tony, holding two drinks, was watching us from a few steps away. He had on a dark gray suit, the coat covering a black shirt open at the neck, no tie. It was a little dressed down for this kind of thing but my first thought was *hawt*.

Wait, had I just thought Tony Reyes looked hot? Our phone conversation and his thank you were messing with my head. I could no longer deny that he actually had human emotions. I felt sorry for him. That was all.

"For you," he said to his daughter, handing her a soda. His eyes met mine. "I didn't know you were going to be here tonight."

I shrugged. "I'm stalking you, obviously."

Vale snorted.

Tony's gaze swept over my short lace dress, down my legs, across my chest, never lingering, but everywhere. Heat flooded my cheeks.

"In that dress, I guess I can forgive it. As long as you don't have a weapon hidden in your lingerie."

"Dad, gross!" Vale said, making a face.

There were so many things I wanted to say, most of them dirty, so I kept them to myself.

"Sorry, sweetheart," he said to Vale. "Just giving Miss Elliot a hard time."

"Well, don't," she replied, "or my party might end up looking like this one."

She gave me a look and we shared a secret smile.

Tony glanced between us. "I'll be on my best behavior."

"You better." Vale craned her neck. "Hey, I think I see Manda." She bolted in less time it took me to apply lip gloss.

Tony stood beside me, watching Vale who was being tackled by another girl. "It's good, someone her own age is here."

"I'm surprised you don't have arm candy dangling from that suit of yours."

"I don't date. Not since Nita."

"Because she was a bag?"

He smiled wryly. "That. And Vale. I'm not going to parade a bunch of women in front of her. I wouldn't introduce her to someone unless things were...serious."

"You have to date for things to get serious."

He tugged at his collar. "What about you? Who are you here with?"

"My father."

It was his turn to look surprised.

"We're very close." Wait, did that sound creepy? People never understood but I hated explaining. "We always have been. Since my mother died. I was around the same age as Vale when I lost her. Not the same thing, but I know what it's like to be a teenage girl without a mother." Whoa, what was up with my word vomit? Just because he'd opened up to me, didn't mean I needed to get all *feelings* and *childhood scarring* with him.

He brushed a strand of hair from my shoulder, leaving a trail of fire in his wake. "What is it like?"

He had to go there. I took a breath, unsettled by his stare. "Very difficult. But I had my dad. He was always there for me. Like you are, for Vale."

He leaned in, cupping my elbow, his body heat causing goose bumps to break out over my arms. He opened his mouth to say something but an arm draped over his shoulder, pulling him away.

"Antonio Reyes. How lovely to see you."

The woman was in her forties, smooth forehead and full lips, not to mention a body like Sofia Vergara. In fact, was it Sofia Vergara?

"Rosana, nice to see you as well," Tony replied.

A doppelgänger then.

"It's been so long," she purred. "We need to catch up."

That was my cue. "Excuse me," I said, surprised the words came out sharp.

I walked away, something boiling under my skin but I wasn't sure what. Not jealousy, surely not. I didn't like Antonio Reyes. It was a mutual feeling, he'd admitted it himself.

It was anger. Anger at being interrupted in the middle of our conversation. Not jealousy, and definitely not attraction. It didn't matter that tonight he looked hot enough to lick. He was old. *Old.* He had wrinkles and gray hair and a very noticeable crease between his eyebrows. I turned back to look.

The woman, Rosana, was playing with his suit jacket, but Tony had one hand in his pocket, the other holding his drink. He was looking away from her. His eyes met mine.

I flushed and turned away. Like a schoolgirl. What was wrong with me?

"Do I look old?" Dad said when I found him. He was checking out his reflection in a spoon. I gently took it from him.

"You have never looked old," I said, "and I am convinced you never will."

"I feel old," he grumbled.

"You're like Benjamin Button, aging in reverse. Trust me."

He kissed me on the cheek. "I couldn't get through these things without you."

"Of course you could."

"Not anymore. Not when I'm the oldest in the room."

Walter Elliot had always been preoccupied with his looks, but I was afraid it was teetering into an obsession. If something was going on with him, he wasn't talking to me about it, and he usually told me everything.

"Who is that?" Dad asked, nodding at the man coming toward us.

My face lifted, but I killed that as soon as I realized. Tony stopped in front of us. "This is my latest client. Antonio Reyes, meet my father, Walter Elliot."

They shook hands and exchanged pleasantries.

"I was wondering if your daughter would dance with me?" Antonio said to Dad. "If you can spare her for a few minutes."

Dad sized him up and down. "I suppose." His voice was neutral, no way to tell what he was thinking.

Tony took my hand and led me to the dance floor. When he pulled me close, his arm around my waist, my pulse jumped. I rolled my eyes.

He caught it. "Is something the matter?"

"No." I bit my lip, uncertain around him for the first time. "You're going above and beyond behaving."

He looked down at me with an eyebrow raised.

"For Vale. You said you would behave around me."

"I will if you will."

His body was close, pressed against mine, our legs almost intertwined. Despite my heart beating, I pushed my chest against him. "But I like giving you a hard time."

His gaze moved to my lips. "I know."

My mind asked what the heck I was doing while my body had other ideas. My lips parted.

Antonio sucked in a breath. "I'm sorry."

Confusion muddled my brain, mixed with desire. Confusion at the desire. "For what?"

"We have a business relationship. My daughter is watching. I don't break these rules."

I frowned. "I don't understand."

His hand tightened on my back. "I like you Elizabeth. I rarely date but I would like to date you. But now is probably not the best time."

My guard was up before I realized I'd dropped it. "Who said I wanted to date you?"

"Elizabeth—"

"What was it, the dancing? The flirting?" I let him go and stepped back. "What exactly did I do to make you think I wanted to be with you?"

"You don't?" he challenged.

"I don't like you, I've always been very clear about that."

The other couples on the dance floor moved away from us.

"You like me more than you know."

My blood raced. "You arrogant b—"

"Let me stop you there so you don't make a scene in public." He leaned close, but didn't touch me. Did I want him to touch me? "Or maybe you should step outside so you can take a breather."

My fists clenched. "I don't need to step outside. I am just fine, *thankyouverymuch*."

He grabbed my elbow, his touch burning. I yanked it out of his grasp and walked away. He followed.

"Dad." Vale met us on the edge of the dance floor. "You didn't ruin it, did you?" She looked between the two of us.

I took a deep breath, then smiled. I was a professional and I would act like one. "We were just having one of our usual disagreements."

"I disagree," Antonio said behind me. "But I should not have said anything. We will forget it ever happened."

"Forgotten," I shot over my shoulder. I told Vale I would see her later and then escaped.

It wasn't forgotten. The press of his body, the way my own had responded. And his words. I didn't want to admit it, but they'd unsettled me.

They'd unraveled me.

CHAPTER 13

Stupid pillow was lumpy. My sheets felt suffocating. Even my mattress was uncomfortable. It was all garbage and in the morning, I'd get rid of everything and buy new.

Or maybe it wasn't my pillow's fault that I couldn't sleep. Thoughts of Antonio muddied my brain, preventing me from relaxing.

As usual, it was all Antonio's fault.

He wanted to date me. He liked me. We had almost kissed, right there in front of Vale and my dad and why hadn't he kissed me?

I knew why. That wasn't the problem. The problem was realizing how badly I wanted it.

Antonio Reyes was not my type. Not only in age and looks, but in personality too. He was so serious. And hard-working. And a great father.

Wait. These weren't necessarily bad things.

But did I want those things? That's what I couldn't figure out. Obviously, I was attracted to him, as much as that still surprised me. Not that he wasn't good looking—he was handsome and sexy and oozing maturity, but not in an old-man way like I first thought. His lips were lush, bordered by a beard barely grown. And his skin, so golden, so beautiful, I wanted to—

I punched my pillow. This was ridiculous. Just an attraction, nothing more. I didn't actually *like* him. I'd told him straight up I didn't. He was annoying and cocky and used to getting his own way...

Just like me.

Opposites were supposed to attract, that's how it had always been for me. But truth was I'd been getting tired of the guys who goofed off all the time. Or the ones who always gave me what I wanted without putting up a fight. I wanted a fight. I wanted to be challenged. I didn't want to be bored any longer, and Antonio wasn't boring.

I *did* like him. And I wanted to date him.

Unfortunately, knowing this was useless since he wouldn't date me. Because of our business relationship, because of Vale.

So I would go on like always, and forget the way my blood ran hot at the thought of him. I would stop wishing that kiss would have happened, stop imagining what it would have been like.

My fingers brushed across my lips. Antonio Reyes. I sighed into my pillow.

After a long day, I grabbed sushi on my way home. Dad was on the balcony when I arrived, watching the sun set over the ocean— one of his favorite things to do. Putting the sushi and some glasses of wine on the table between us, I sat down and reveled in the quiet. The lack of ringing phones, the stress of the day melting away, the relief that despite my family's many issues, having a parent like Nita Oliver wasn't one of them.

"I'm exhausted," I said, dipping a piece of sushi in soy sauce. It didn't help that I hadn't gotten any sleep last night.

"You work too hard," Dad replied. "May I?" He motioned at the sushi.

"Of course."

"I shouldn't eat too much, I'm having work done tomorrow."

I frowned. "What? Like botox?"

Dad looked at me sideways. "Among other things."

"Dad, why? You look great."

He smiled and patted my arm but didn't reply.

"Seriously. You don't need work done." Sure, he was getting older, but he was in his sixties after all. Too much botox and he'd start looking creepy.

Dad stared out at the ocean. The sun cast a pinkish glow over his face. "I can't keep up with the younger men anymore. You should see the other Botticelli For Men models. They make me feel so…"

He didn't need to finish, we could both hear the word.

"Are you talking about your new ad campaign?"

"They have me standing in the middle of all these twenty-somethings. I look like a grandfather."

"You are a grandfather."

He grimaced. "I'm done shooting this ad, but if I want to land another contract, I need to have some procedures done."

I munched another piece of sushi. "If that's what you really want. But I still think you're the handsomest man I've ever seen."

Dad smiled. "You have to say that."

"I really don't. And it's still true."

He grabbed my hand. "Sweetheart, you've always been more than my daughter. You've been my joy, my best friend, my companion. You're always there for me."

This talk was freaking me out a bit—Dad rarely got sappy. "What's your point, Dad?"

He let go of my hand, swung his legs to the side of the chair and faced me. He rested his elbows on his knees. "No man is worthy of you, in my eyes. But I'm worried that, because I feel this way, you've never gotten close to a man before."

"I've had lots of boyfriends—"

"I know. Boyfriends." His mouth twisted around the word.

"But I worry about you sometimes. Maybe I'm holding you back from the love you deserve."

"Not true." Truth was, I'd never found a man I loved that much. Either they didn't stick around or I got bored. Men, friends, shoes, handbags… I felt the same about them all—sick of it after a few months. Ready for something new. It would be the same with Antonio—wasn't it better if we never gave it a try?

"I want you to be happy."

"I am happy," I said. But I didn't smile. Was I happy? Was this the happiest people got? Or was there more? I honestly didn't know. But I felt happy enough.

"Well." He patted his knees then stood. "I better turn in early. I'll be in the clinic most of the day tomorrow."

"Call me when you're done, okay?" I said. "I'll pick you up."

"Thank you, sweetheart." He kissed the top of my head. "Night."

"See you tomorrow," I called after him.

CHAPTER 14

I'D ALREADY BEEN BUZZED THROUGH THE GATE, SO I DIDN'T KNOW what was taking Ava so long. Power move maybe, making me, the older sister, wait on the front steps of her lavish Spanish-style mansion as if reminding me she had everything while I had…less. Hopefully that ridiculously hot husband of hers wasn't home, I really didn't want to see him—

"Beth." Eric covered the doorway all tall and blond and cut, the perfect amount of muscle showing through his shirt and a wary look on his face. This is why I hated him. Because he was gorgeous and he'd never once seen me as anything other than Ava's sister.

"Eric." I pushed past him inside, the bowl clutched in my arms.

"Come on in," he said, his voice dry.

"Where is she?" My sister didn't even have the decency to greet me?

"She's in the—"

"I'm in the kitchen!" Ava yelled, speaking over her husband.

I clacked my way across the floor, not bothering to worry whether my heels were making little dents in the wood.

"Hey, Beth," Ava said, turning from the kitchen sink. She held a washcloth and a pot, carefully keeping them over the sink so they wouldn't drip water onto the floor. "What's up?"

Eric picked up a towel and joined Ava at the sink. He rested his hand on her hip and she leaned into him.

"I brought back this bowl of yours since you couldn't be bothered to come get it." I set it on the counter.

She gave me a blank look.

"From when you made that disgusting meatless chili at our last family dinner?"

Eric's eyes narrowed on me, reproachful. Ava didn't notice.

"Right! Thanks." She brushed a strand of hair from her face with the back of her wrist. "Sorry, I forgot all about it."

I rolled my eyes. "Yes, I'm sure your oh-so-busy schedule—"

"If you've come over just to insult my wife," Eric said, throwing the dishtowel over his shoulder like he was about to throw down, "you can leave now."

Ava nudged him in the ribs. "Stop."

An entire conversation seemed to pass between them with one look. It was maddening. Everything about them drove me crazy. I didn't even know why I'd come in the first place. Who cared about the stupid bowl? Now was the time to turn around and leave.

I leaned my palms against the counter. "Who does dishes anymore, anyway?"

Ava went back to scrubbing. "Our dishwasher broke. The new one isn't getting delivered until this afternoon."

Ugh, how menial. I'd let the dishes pile up rather than washing them *by hand*.

Ava drained the sink, squeezing the cloth out and resting it over the tap. She turned to me. "Whatever happened with that guy?"

"What guy?"

She went to the fridge and grabbed a sparkling water, then handed it to me. "The one who ruined one of your parties but then wanted to hire you?"

I blinked, surprised she'd remembered. "He's a client. The party is coming up soon."

She smiled, and I wanted to wipe it off her face it was so... proud. Like I'd done the right thing.

I took a sip of water, telling myself to relax. I'd been such a bag to Ava for so long, it was an automatic reaction. One I swear I was trying to break.

"How's it going?" Ava asked.

Eric pressed himself beside her, his arm going around her waist and lips brushing a kiss against her temple before looking at me. Both of them stood there, waiting for me to talk to them, to tell them about my life as if they actually cared. And, I had to grudgingly admit, they probably did. Or, at least, Ava did.

"It's going fine." I turned away, wishing I could open up to my sister but knowing I wouldn't. Couldn't. "I should go."

Ava walked me to the door. "Thanks for bringing the bowl back."

I left without a reply. I could imagine what Ava would do now. She'd walk back into the kitchen where Eric was waiting. He'd pull her close and they'd kiss, not the lustful kind of new relationships but a deep and lasting kind. The kind of kiss that wasn't the start or the end but a continuation of what was already there and would always be there.

The kind of kiss I'd never really had. The kind of kiss I wanted.

As I pulled out of their driveway, it was annoyingly clear why I hated going there. Jealousy, plain and simple. Not of the Spanish-style house because I preferred modern, and not of Eric, because despite his hotness he'd always seemed a bit too vanilla for me. I was jealous of what they had together. What they were to each other.

I wanted it, and I wanted it with Antonio. Maybe it wouldn't work out with us, but for the first time ever, the risk seemed worth it.

I rang the doorbell. Anxiety rippled through me, threatening to stain my armpits or redden my face. But I was Elizabeth Elliot and I did not get sweat stains.

Vale answered the door. "Beth! Come on in."

I followed her inside, my heels loud on the floor. I winced at the sound but I wasn't sorry. Killer heels are a must when you're about to tell a man you're into him.

"Everything is pretty much set, right?" Vale asked, leading me into the kitchen.

"Yep. I just want to confirm everything, see to any last-minute changes, that kind of thing." A total excuse.

I spread the portfolio onto the kitchen table, papers and pictures and lists and order forms. Juliet had everything stored digitally, but I preferred hard copies in my hand.

Vale picked up a picture of the centerpiece she'd designed. She practically sighed, in a good way. "I can't believe it's next weekend."

"Time flies and all that," I said, distracted. Where was Antonio? It was possible he didn't want to see me. We'd spoken a few times since I'd flipped on him at the party, but always on the phone and always formal and polite. What I wanted to say had to be said in person.

"Almost everyone is coming," Vale said. "Oh, and there are a few people I invited spur-of-the-moment."

I contained a groan. "How many?"

"Don't worry. I made a list." She grinned.

The little imp. She knew just how to work me. Spring additional guests but soften the blow with a list. I loved lists. Everything was better with a list.

"It's in my room, I'll go grab it," she said. Then, "Hey, Dad."

I stiffened. My back was to him but I heard Vale's footsteps disappear. Or maybe that was him, unwilling to be in a room alone with me.

I turned. Antonio was staring at me. His eyes took me in and I knew the outfit I'd chosen was a hit.

"Elizabeth."

He said my name with a bit of an accent. I'd never noticed before how sexy it sounded.

"Antonio." I was gripping one of my precious lists. I set it down carefully on the table. It was now or never. Vale would be back in minutes and I needed to make use of this alone time.

"I wanted to…" This was harder than I thought. I didn't have much practice with apologies. "I want to apologize."

His eyebrows rose. "This seems like a momentous occasion. Maybe I should sit down."

I pursed my lips, trying not to rise to his bait. "Not necessary."

He leaned his hip against the counter, waiting for me to go on. Being in the kitchen with him made me think of Ava and Eric—their casual yet constant touching.

"I'm sorry for the other night. I…overreacted. I was impolite."

He cocked his head and I took that as an invitation to move closer.

"You caught me off guard." I ran my hand along the smooth marble counter beside me, wishing I was touching his crisp white shirt instead.

"I don't know how to be shy about my feelings," he said.

And I didn't know how to be so open. I was right in front of him now, only a breath of space between us. He glanced at my lips, then back into my eyes.

My voice was breathy when I said, "You were right."

"Was I?" His head tilted nearer.

"Yes." Yes, he was right, and yes please kiss me right now. I licked my lips.

He made a sound deep in his throat. "About?"

I opened my mouth, ready to tell him I wanted to be with him, even if we had to wait until the party was over. Ready for him to take my lips in his. Ready.

"Mom?"

I blinked. His head reared back. We stared at each other in

confusion for a few moments before we heard footsteps drawing near.

"Mom, what are you doing here?"

Antonio whipped around just as Vale followed a woman into the kitchen.

With a big smile, she reached for Vale and Antonio at the same time, pulling Vale into her side. Antonio didn't move.

"Tony," she said. "Did you miss me?"

CHAPTER 15

I'D GONE INVISIBLE. AND I HATED IT.

"Nita. What are you doing here?" Antonio did not sound pleased.

So this was the famous Nita. I sized her up. She was tall and slim, built like a model except for her chest which was obviously man made. Her face had that "done" look about it, the mark of plastic surgery. But her hair...I envied that hair. Long and thick, black as night and super glossy. Maybe it was a wig.

"Mom?" Vale asked.

"My daughter turns sixteen only once. I couldn't miss it." She tugged Vale closer in a sign of affection, but she was staring at Antonio.

He glanced at me, a flicker of his eyebrows betraying his thoughts. To me anyway. He thought I'd told her about the party. I'd written the address wrong, the invite shouldn't have made it to her. Unless Vale told her after all.

Nita let Vale go. She brushed past Antonio, trailing a finger across his shoulders. He flinched.

She stopped at the kitchen table and perused the contents of my portfolio. "Are you throwing a party?" Her eyes met mine, her first acknowledgement of my presence. "Who is this?"

Antonio threw me a glance again.

"This is Elizabeth, our party planner," Vale answered. "We sent you an invitation. Isn't that why you're here?"

Nita cocked her head. "I never received an invitation."

Silence was thick in the room. "It's in the mail," I said innocently.

Her mouth tightened. Then she shrugged. "No matter. I'm here now."

Antonio was silent.

"The party isn't until next weekend," Vale said. "But everything is planned. Doesn't it look great? Beth is awesome!" She threw her arm over my shoulder. Nita's gaze sharpened before she dropped it back to my portfolio.

"This all looks fine, I suppose," she drawled.

I stiffened.

"But the theme? It's so country." She tossed some of the papers back onto the table and they went sliding to the floor. "Vale. You're turning sixteen. This is an important occasion, not a little girl's dress-up party."

Vale's face turned red.

"No offense to your party planner—"

My fists clenched.

"—but we're throwing this out and starting over."

"Excuse me?" I said.

She gave me a thin-lipped smile. "We won't be needing you anymore. Tony will pay for whatever you've done so far, but I can take it from here."

Vale looked on the verge of tears. "But, Mom—"

This woman was a piece of work. Why Antonio had married her in the first place was a mystery. Even more a mystery? Why he wasn't speaking up.

"This party is exactly what Vale wants," I said.

Nita's eyes flashed. "Valentina doesn't know what she wants.

But I know my daughter better than some *party planner*." She said it like I was the dirt under her fingernails. She picked up the picture of Vale's centerpieces. "I will give my daughter a proper birthday party. Not this tacky excuse for a Sweet Sixteen."

Vale's eyes welled.

I yanked the paper from Nita. "We have a contract."

She waved her hand. "Contracts can be broken, for the right price."

"Nita." Tony's voice cracked like a whip, silencing us both. "Get out of my house."

"Dad, no. Please." Vale stood in front of her mother, as if to shield her. I had no clue why, especially after what her mother had just said.

"Our house." Nita put her arms around her daughter, resting her chin on Vale's shoulder. "And Valentina wants me to stay."

I waited for Antonio to make her leave. Drag her by that glossy hair if he had to. I'd pay good money to see that, in fact. But he pinched the bridge of his nose, his teeth grinding.

He couldn't possibly listen to this woman. After all the work I'd done, after the way she had just treated Vale. Like a pawn in her game.

"Antonio."

No. I had not just said his name like that, like I was begging for him to be on my side.

His hand dropped, he looked at Vale. "Is this what you want?"

Nita laughed. She moved around Vale and toward her ex-husband. "Of course it is." She draped herself on him, as if trying to convince him it was what he wanted, too.

"Vale?" he asked.

Vale half-turned to me, her face apologetic. "I don't want Mom to leave."

"Excellent. I'll get right to work, I don't have much time." She patted Vale on the cheek. "Don't worry about a thing, sweetheart, I'll plan a Sweet Sixteen any girl would die for."

Just like that, I was fired.

I quickly gathered up my things. I didn't want to be in that house any longer. Not around Vale, who'd become like a friend to me, a little sister, a daughter? Or around Antonio, who had chosen his ex, the woman who'd cheated on him and treated their daughter like dirt, over me.

"Beth," Vale whispered. "I'm sorry. I..."

"No need," I snapped. Tears filled Vale's eyes. I turned away from them.

"If you could leave me the guest list before you go," Nita said as I was leaving the kitchen.

Ripping her hair out, that sounded like a fantastic idea. I spun around, ready to tell her to shove it, when I caught Vale's face. This wasn't about me, it was about her. Nita had already damaged Vale's vision of her Sweet Sixteen, I wouldn't make it any worse.

Oh how I hated being mature. And kind. It was much more fun to be vindictive and petty.

I pulled a sheet of paper from my portfolio but I didn't give it to Nita when she held her hand out. Instead, I placed it on the counter and turned away. There. A tiny bit of pettiness felt good.

I marched to the front door, my heels noisy on the floor. How different I felt now than I did barely a half hour ago. Before, anxious and excited. Hopeful. Now...angry.

"Elizabeth." Antonio called my name but I didn't turn. "Elizabeth, wait."

I was done with this family. I'd have Juliet work out how much he owed me, plus extra for breaking our contract, but I had no interest in talking to him again.

"Please," he said, reaching the door at the same time as me. "I—"

"I'll send you the bill."

I left without looking back.

CHAPTER 16

I took a spa day. That way I wouldn't have to purposely ignore the buzz of my cell every five minutes. At the spa, my phone stayed in a locker where it could vibrate up the wazoo without annoying anyone.

After my relaxing day which didn't relax me at all, I checked my notifications on the way to my car. Ten calls from Juliet. Six from Antonio. One from Vale. One from my sister Ava. And one from an unknown number. About a zillion texts, all telling me to call someone right away.

I listened to my messages. Juliet wanted details about what happened with the Reyes account. She also had a couple of possible new clients she wanted to discuss. I wasn't in the mood.

Vale's message was short. "I'm sorry. Your party was everything I wanted and I loved it. But my mom... I'm sorry."

From Antonio: "Elizabeth." His voice sent every nerve in my body on high alert. "I apologize for yesterday. Usually, I don't handle my business affairs in that manner, but the party is for Vale and I told you from the start that I will adhere to her wishes. I've already spoken with your assistant Jules, and she will deduct the amount from my credit card. Goodbye."

So cold. So formal. And nothing about that thing between us. Nothing except a lifeless apology. At least I'd get some money out of the whole thing. Enough to break even on my outstanding bills, or so Juliet said.

Stupid Tony Reyes. I wish I'd never met him.

The next message stopped me cold: "Hi, this is Emilia Ackers calling for Elizabeth Elliot. I'm a nurse at Cedars-Sinai. Your father is in serious condition. If you could come as soon as you can, I will give you the details when you arrive."

Panic pounded inside my chest making it hard to breathe. I started the car and peeled out of the lot.

Stupid spa day. Stupid me for taking a spa day. I glanced at the phone to see when the nurse had called. Two hours ago. I spat out a curse and rammed my foot on the gas pedal. At a stoplight, I listened to the last message, the one from my sister. "Beth, it's Ava. I got a call saying Dad is in the hospital. Cedars-Sinai. I'm heading over there now. You're probably already there, but I called in case you didn't know or in case... Just come."

Ava sounded as frantic as I felt.

When I finally found his floor, Ava was sitting in the waiting room, her head in her hands.

"What happened?" I demanded. "He's okay, right?"

She lifted her head. Tears had smudged her mascara. Her face was red and puffy. She pulled me into a hug.

I stiffened, then relaxed.

"I'm glad you're here," she said, letting me go. "He had an infection that led to septic shock."

"What does that mean? Can I see him?"

She shook her head. "He's gone into surgery. To get rid of the infection." She slumped back into the chair.

"How did this happen?" I sat beside her, staring at the nurse's desk in front of me but not really seeing it. My father was in surgery. Septic shock. I didn't know what that meant but it was obviously worse than it sounded.

"Botched plastic surgery." Ava's words were flat.

I closed my eyes. Of all the stupid... But it wasn't stupid to Dad. His looks were important to him. These days, they were his main source of income.

"Did you know?" Ava asked. Despite her words, there was no accusation to her tone.

"That he was getting work done? Yeah, he told me." I glanced at her. "He didn't tell me what he was getting done though. He was pretty mum about it all."

Ava raised an eyebrow and I knew what that meant. She was surprised Dad hadn't confided in me.

"Apparently, the clinic he went to has a bad reputation," she said.

"What?" Dad would never go to a place that didn't deliver top-notch results. He wouldn't risk it.

"I don't think Dad knew." Ava ran her hands over her thighs. She had on jeans and a t-shirt, flip flops, and her hair was in a ponytail. Not exactly the right look for the wife of a famous singer. What if the paparazzi found her? "One of the nurses told me it's a place that's all about get in, get out. The price is right—not too cheap to be suspicious but not over the top—but their doctors aren't the most reputable."

"How could Dad not have known?"

"They cover their tracks. Glowing reviews on their website, the clinic is fancy from what the nurse said. Some of the doctors and nurses know, but they can't shut it down."

"Well, they should," I snapped. "If they would only do their job, Dad wouldn't be in surgery right now."

Ava squeezed my hand but I wrenched it from her grasp.

I knew it wasn't their fault, but I needed someone to blame. Like the person who had operated on him. "Did you talk to him? Did he tell you the name of his doctor? Because we should sue. We're going to sue."

"I haven't been able to see him yet," she said.

"When I find out who did this..."

"Beth."

I'd gotten out of my chair without realizing. But I hated sitting there doing nothing. If I couldn't see Dad, I wanted to find the person responsible and stab a needle up their nose.

"Beth, we'll worry about that later. Right now we need to be here when Dad gets out of surgery."

I glared. I hated being told what to do, especially by my younger sister. I hated it even more when she was right.

"Beth, please." Ava reached out for me, then dropped her hand. "Dad needs you."

"Of course he does," I grumbled as I sat back down. "He needs me more than you."

The corner of Ava's mouth twitched. "I know."

When Dad came out of it, I would be the first face he saw. That's the way he would want it.

"I'm glad you're here," Ava said softly.

I would never admit it out loud, but I was glad she was there too.

CHAPTER 17

WALTER ELLIOT HAD NEVER LOOKED SO OLD, OR SO FRAIL. LINES etched his face, deeper than they'd ever been, purple bags drooped under his eyes.

"Dad?" I kept my voice low.

"Sweetheart." His lips, red and puffy, gave a small grin.

I sat on the chair beside his bed and took his hand in mine. "How are you feeling?"

"Oh, I don't feel so bad. Exhausted. The pain is manageable."

At least there was that.

"The better question is, how do I look?"

To lie or not to lie? Dad would look in the mirror soon enough —in fact I was surprised he hadn't already demanded one.

"You've looked better."

He grimaced. "That bad?" When I wouldn't meet his eyes, he gave my hand a gentle squeeze. "Please, precious daughter, give it to me straight."

I met his gaze. "Pretty bad."

"I thought so. My face feels like it's been stung by a million bees. My stomach...well never mind my stomach." He touched his skin with his fingertips, the IV tube stretching across the bed.

His face was puffy, but it was the surgery that concerned me more. "What about the rest of you?" I asked. "Are you going to recover okay?"

"Oh, sure. Doc said they fixed the damage done, got rid of the infection. I have to stay a couple of days so they can pump me with meds and fluids."

I frowned. "As soon as you can, I want you to give me the name of the quack at that clinic who worked on you. I've already made a list of possible lawyers."

Dad patted my hand. "Sweetheart, don't worry about that."

"No way am I going to let them get away with this!"

"Nor will I. But I will take care of it." His voice was firm. "You have a job to get back to. I will handle this when I get out."

I didn't want to tell my father I had no job right now. Juliet wanted to set up a new client, but there was no way I could even think about a party. Not with my dad in the hospital, not after what happened with my last client.

"What's wrong?" he asked.

"I'm worried about you." It was halfway true. "If I lost you…" My throat closed and I clenched my teeth. Anger was better than sappiness. "Don't ever do this to me again."

His lips curled. "I will make that promise, but you have to promise something in return."

I waited.

"I promise no more plastic surgery, unless it's something minor, like Botox, and only from a reputable doctor."

"That's not very reassuring."

"Too bad, that's what you're going to get."

"And what do I have to agree to?"

"You will promise to have more fun. Don't worry about me so much. Go out with that Spanish man you were dancing with the other night. What was his name, Alejandro?"

"Antonio," I whispered.

"You have feelings for him. Seeing you together, I could tell."

"But—"

"No excuses. He may look a bit weathered, but he's handsome enough. And if he makes you happy, honestly I don't care that he doesn't use night cream. Maybe I can get him to try Botticelli For Men. Wouldn't hurt my chances for another ad campaign."

Dad continued to talk but I was finding it hard to breathe. My heart was racing faster than my sister Mari at a sample sale. My hands began to shake.

"Elizabeth, are you okay?"

I gasped for breath. If I was having a heart attack, at least I was in a hospital. "I'm fine. I probably just need some coffee." I stood. "Ava's been waiting to see you, I'll send her in."

Outside his room, I leaned against the wall and closed my eyes.

"What's wrong?" Ava asked. "Is Dad okay?"

"He's fine. But I think I'm having a heart attack."

She raised her eyebrows. "Should I get a nurse?"

I ignored the dryness in her tone. "Never mind, I'm better now." Not a heart attack but maybe a panic attack. Some kind of attack. "I'm going home to freshen up, then I'll be back."

Ava said something in reply but I was already too far gone to hear.

At home, I stood in the shower, my forehead against the tile while the hot water ran down my body. Dad had spoken of Antonio so casually. Had he actually seen something between us, when I hadn't known it existed at the time?

Not that it mattered, because whatever had been there was gone. It was all just a might have been now, nothing more than a fantasy.

Me, walking down the street with Antonio, our hands clasped. Laughing, our faces glowing. Happy.

And Vale, walking next to me. Her arm linked with mine. A family.

I shivered despite the heat. I never knew I wanted that, not with them, not with anyone. Dad had always been enough, my two sisters plenty.

But now that they were gone—this imaginary family where I was the center—I wanted it. I ached for it. I missed Vale. I missed Antonio. I missed how we were together, the texts, the laughter, the banter. I missed the possibilities.

Tears broke free, mixing with the water streaming over my face. I sobbed like I hadn't since my mother died. Feelings I never allowed myself to have threatened to drown me. This is what caring got me. This pain was why I didn't open myself up to anyone. Life was much easier when my Dad was the only one who owned a part of my heart.

I didn't know when I had started letting people in but I hated myself for it. Hated my vulnerability. But I cried anyway, because no one was there to see.

CHAPTER 18

THE ACHE OF MISSING ANTONIO AND VALE DIDN'T GO AWAY. I KNEW it would eventually, but I also knew I didn't want it to. I wanted them in my life, and it was up to me to make that happen.

But I wasn't quite ready for a face-to-face. So, baby steps. I called Vale, knowing she wouldn't answer—she only answered texts—but she'd get the message.

"Hi, Vale," I said after her recording. "It's Elizabeth." I hesitated. I'd planned all these things I was going to say, but now couldn't remember any of them. "I just wanted to say I'm sorry for not returning your texts, and mostly I'm sorry that I'm not working with you on the party anymore. Not because of the money, or anything, but...I..."

I couldn't tell her I missed her, like she was my only friend or something. She was a teenage girl and I was an adult. I had more pride than that.

"...I loved planning the party with you. And your father. He..."

I was bad at this.

"Anyway, if you need any help at all with the party, I'm here for you. I know your mom is planning everything now, but I can help. If you need me. Not as an official party planner but as a friend. Okay, bye."

I clicked end and then pressed the phone against my forehead. Smooth, Beth. Really smooth. I sounded like a fourteen-year-old missing her BFF.

On my phone, I pulled up my call list and stared at Antonio's name. So many calls I'd made to him, or him to me. How many times had we talked, or argued?

My finger hovered over his name.

I turned my phone off.

"I'm sorry to call you while you're at the hospital."

I left Dad's room. Ava was in there anyway, telling Dad all about Eric's latest album. Or in other words, blah blah blah look at my rich and famous husband blah blah.

"It's okay."

"Is your father doing better?" Juliet asked.

I leaned against the white wall. "He's recovering." Dad would be fine. A day or two more and he'd be out of there and back home where he belonged.

"We need to talk about these two new contracts. Will you come into the office as soon as you can?"

I sighed. Juliet was right, I couldn't ignore work forever. There would come a day when I wanted it back. I couldn't let my hard-earned business go bust because I wasn't feeling it.

"Are they both within the same time frame?" I asked.

"Pretty much. They'd overlap. One is a bigger affair, I don't think we could do both."

"But you have reservations about the bigger party?"

She hesitated, as if wondering how I knew, but it was obvious. If the bigger contract was cut and dry, she'd push for that one. "The woman seems like she'd be...difficult to work with. I don't know if it would be worth it."

84

I knew difficult. I was difficult, I could handle it. I told Juliet so.

"I know, but I thought, with everything going on right now, maybe you wouldn't want to take on a client like this."

I stared at my bare toes, desperately in need of a pedicure. I was spending most of my time at the hospital because I didn't want Dad to be alone. And it always felt safe with him, familiar. Comforting, despite the sterile décor and smell of sick people and bleach.

"I don't know when I'm going to make it into the office," I said.

"But—"

"We need a contract. I know." I took a breath. "Jules, I think you should make the decision."

The phone was silent. For a long time. "Jules?" I said.

"You called me by my name."

I rolled my eyes. "Decide which party is better for us, then let me know. My dad should be home in a couple of days and then I can jump into work. But we need to choose before they both decide to go somewhere else."

"Okay." She didn't sound sure, which was hardly comforting.

"Don't wimp out on me now," I said, peering into Dad's room. He'd fallen asleep. "Decide. But make the right decision."

When Ava spotted me, she tiptoed out.

"You were that boring, huh?" I asked Ava, while waiting for Juliet to respond. Maybe I'd freaked Jules out so bad she was finally going to crack. I thought the girl was made of stronger stuff, to be honest.

"He's tired," Ava said. "I thought we could go get lunch. But if you'd rather make fun of me and eat alone…"

"Let's eat at A.O.C. I'll drive."

"Elizabeth?" Jules cut in.

"Are you going to do this or not?" I asked her.

"Yes."

"Good." I hesitated, turning away from Ava. If I was being honest with myself and with Vale, I could with Jules as well. "You're an excellent assistant, Jules. Pick the event, get started on the preliminary planning, and then maybe we'll discuss a raise. A small one. Like fifty cents or something."

I wasn't *her* freaking fairy godmother after all.

"Understood," she replied. "I'll email you the details. And thank you for the opportunity."

I hung up, then turned to my sister. "Let's go. And you're paying. Not all of us have a rich husband."

CHAPTER 19

WE SAT OUTSIDE ON THE PATIO OF A.O.C., THE LOS ANGELES weather a perfect mix of warm sun and light breeze. Ava spent the first ten minutes on the phone with her husband, making gooey noises and threatening to ruin my appetite. Not that we could order while she was so preoccupied.

"So, is he leaving you for a younger, hotter woman?" I asked when she'd hung up.

She shot me a look.

"Sorry. Old habits and all that."

"Well, don't make me relive them," she replied, "or you'll be eating alone. And paying."

"Threats are new for you."

She pursed her lips but didn't say anything. Ava had always been like that. While it was a chore for me to keep my filter on, Ava usually kept her thoughts to herself. I'd been working on that, but it wasn't much fun.

After we ordered, an awkwardness settled between us. Ava and I didn't spend much time together. Sure, we'd both been at the hospital these last few days. We'd lived in the same house for years. She helped me plan the *Pillow Talk* party. We spent time together when there was a reason to, rarely just because.

"When Dad was awake, he couldn't stop talking about **Excessively Diverted**," Ava said. "He's really proud."

Not the topic I wanted to go with. "It's…yeah." I loved the job, but I'd lost my love for the job.

"Come on," she said. "Throw me a bone here."

I took a sip of my sparkling water. "It's a great job." I said without conviction.

"I bet you're fabulous at it."

I raised an eyebrow at her.

"What? The *Pillow Talk* party you threw was a huge success. I remember how great you were at planning the whole thing. I could never put together something like that."

My shoulders were tense, but I forced them to relax. This was my sister. Her compliments shouldn't make me so uncomfortable.

"I love it. I really do," I said. "I mean, it's fun. And seeing people happy at something I put together? I never thought that would mean so much to me, but it does."

"I bet."

I hesitated. Ava would listen if I told her about Antonio and Vale. She would offer advice, and good advice at that. But did I want to hear it? I wasn't sure I was ready for that yet. I smoothed my hands over the wooden table in front of me. Ava waited patiently. She didn't push. I found I wanted to tell her.

"It's just—"

"Elizabeth."

My whole body stiffened at the sound of his voice.

"Elizabeth, I need to talk to you."

Ava was staring at Antonio, who loomed over my shoulder. I didn't turn around.

"Elizabeth," he said again, my old-fashioned name so sexy coming from his lips. "Please."

Goosebumps erupted from my skin. My eyes met Ava's and she gave me a questioning look.

"Fine." Antonio grabbed a chair from a nearby table, the legs scraping against the ground as he dragged it over. He placed it between me and Ava and sat down.

He nodded at Ava. "Antonio Reyes, nice to meet you."

"Ava Elliot-Wentworth." They shook hands.

Enough small talk. "How did you know I was here?" I demanded.

His eyes burned into me while his voice was calm. "I called your office. Jules told me."

"She can forget about that raise," I mumbled.

"Elizabeth—"

"I want you to leave."

"Nita's gone."

I blinked.

"She spent a day planning this completely glitzy, over-the-top disco party, ignoring everything Valentina said to her. And then she basically quit. Told us everything would work itself out. Spent her time ignoring Vale while trying to get back together with me. Vale finally had it and told her to leave."

My emotions were a mixed bag. Just what had Nita done to try and get Antonio back? Good for Vale for standing up to that horrible woman. And disco? Please.

He clasped his hands on the tabletop. "We need you. The party is this weekend. You sent the invitations, we never moved the date, and Vale didn't let anyone know the change of theme. I don't know if you can make it work, or if we should postpone, but we need your help on this. Vale needs your help."

His words, his tone of voice, everything was so clinical. Businesslike. As if nothing had happened. Now, the only thing between us was an ever-widening space.

"Why didn't she call me?" I'd already told her I'd help if she needed me. Antonio wouldn't be there asking, unless he had more to say.

"She's embarrassed. Don't tell her I said that to you. She feels badly about what happened that day when Nita showed up. She doesn't know how to talk to you."

I must've been giving him a look because he said, "She's fifteen. As mature as Valentina can be, she's still only a child."

The waitress chose this moment to deliver our food. She glanced at Antonio and her face flushed. "You have another guest. Would you like a menu?" she asked.

"No," he replied. "I'm not staying."

While the waitress asked if he wanted something to drink, I looked across the table at Ava. Her face was carefully blank, but she was probably confused. I couldn't tell her in front of Antonio, and I would never admit it anyway, but I desperately needed her advice.

When the waitress left, Antonio turned back to me. "I apologize again for the way you were dismissed. We... Vale really wants you back."

"I'll have to work overtime to make it happen this weekend."

"I'll pay double."

Despite not having anything in my mouth, I almost choked. I stabbed my fork into a spear of asparagus. The nerve, that he thought paying me double would get me back just like that. Like I could be bought.

Double.

"She says yes."

This time I did choke. And splutter. Ava ignored the daggers I glared at her.

"Beth is the best, and I know she can get it done."

Antonio nodded at Ava but waited for my say so.

I swallowed. Shooting one last evil eye at Ava, I held out my hand to Antonio. "I'll have Jules send you a new contract within the hour, but consider this a verbal agreement."

His lips quirked. "As if I would ever try to stiff you."

I looked away. "You should go. I have a lot of work to do."

His smile dying, he stood. "I'll let Valentina know." He buttoned his suit jacket. "Thank you, Elizabeth."

I took a big bite of my chicken, ignoring him. Ava's eyes followed him as he walked away. When I knew he was gone, the cool and calm demeanor I'd struggled to uphold disappeared.

Ava was looking at me, probably waiting for an explanation.

"Help?" is what she got instead.

CHAPTER 20

WE WORKED AROUND THE CLOCK—JULES AND ME, AND AVA WHEN she wasn't teaching. I barely slept. Jules juggled both the Reyes party, plus putting together a portfolio for our newest client—a retirement party hosted by a small business. Ava did whatever I asked. I might've gotten pleasure out of seeing her jump at my bidding, but I was too busy.

Everything that we'd cancelled had to be rebooked or reordered. Deliveries had to happen immediately so we could start decorating. The catering company I'd originally hired agreed to come back on, but only if we could find them extra cooks. The flower shop delivered all the flowers we wanted, but loose, and I had no one to make the centerpieces Vale designed, or the wreathes and garlands I had planned to adorn the tent and chairs. Jules was a fixture at the Reyes house, there to approve every delivery while struggling with the centerpieces. Finally, Ava brought in some of her teacher friends to make them, giving Jules time to work on the new portfolio.

I pressed send on the email reminder for the guests. Usually I didn't do that kind of thing, but I was worried with the last-minute party change that people might not come in costume.

I checked my notes. Vale's dress was almost done. The seamstress had never stopped working on it because I'd never told her to. I'd planned on giving the dress to Vale as a birthday present anyway. My dress was a no-go. It was way too elaborate to be done on time.

Ava popped her head into my office as I was searching online for something to wear. "What's next?"

Despite juggling this job and her classes, Ava looked fresh and chipper, her skin and hair flawless. My lip curled.

"What?" she asked. "What do you need?"

"Nothing." I rubbed my temples. "A dress."

She leaned against the doorframe. "For you?"

I nodded.

"I know a stylist. I use her every once in awhile when Eric has big events."

Was she trying to make me jealous?

"I can get her on the phone for you. She can find what you're looking for."

"Anything?" The gown I'd planned to wear was fit for royalty. It was very Queen Elizabeth but without the weird neck ruff thing. But maybe I didn't need to go so over the top.

Ava was already dialing on her cell phone. "Zoya? It's Ava Elliot-Wentworth... Yes, but it's not for me, it's for my sister. Is that okay? Here, I'll put her on the phone."

She handed it to me.

I took it, mouthing 'thank you' to my sister who deserved a million thank you's for what she'd done for me these past couple of days. One was all I could spare.

* * *

I smoothed my dress over my hips. It was navy blue, off one shoulder, with a jewelled corset cinching my waist, the skirt flowing from there. The sleeves had a slit down the middle, cinching around my wrists. I kept my hair loose, my makeup simple. The whole look was understated, especially for me, but this wasn't my party. Today was all about Vale.

Everyone was enjoying the party, the food was disappearing faster than the caterers could replenish it, the music was light and fun—kids dancing and twirling on the floor we'd brought in. Vale glowed under the attention and the lights, smiling bigger than I'd ever seen. Friends gathered around her; boys watched her from the sidelines, the braver ones kissing her hand like she was a princess. Which she was right then, in that moment, that night.

That was why I loved my job. Knowing I made someone feel that, even for just one party. Giving them a night they would never forget.

"Are you Elizabeth Elliot?" a woman asked me. She had on a medieval looking gown, her hair covered by a circlet and veil.

"That's me," I replied. The party-planning angel.

She held out her hand. "I'm Maria DeCosta, a friend of Antonio's. This party is incredible. Do you have a card? I'd definitely like to contact you for my annual Christmas party. It's gotten tired. I feel like you could freshen it up."

"Thank you," I said, handing her my card. I'd lost track of how many I'd handed out. Almost every adult at the party had asked for it, some of the teenagers too, begging me to plan their Sweet Sixteen's or Graduation parties.

"How did Antonio find you?" she asked. "Was it a lucky chance?"

Luck, fate, I didn't know what to call it. "Word of mouth."

"I can see why."

"Thank you again, but I should go check on the drinks." It was an excuse, but just then I'd spotted Antonio, making his way toward us.

I'd been avoiding him all night, unsure what to say, how to act. I was no longer angry, just…sad. Hollow, like something had been taken away.

It didn't help that he looked sublimely gorgeous. He'd adamantly refused to dress up, or so he said a few weeks ago. But there he was, head to toe in dark brown leather. His pants were tucked into tall boots; he had on an embellished coat, closed at the waist but with an open collar, showing a white linen shirt underneath. And from his shoulder swung a cape. A cape. It could've been ridiculous, but *dayum*.

I ducked away from the party, popping into the kitchen to make sure everything was running smoothly, that dessert was almost ready, checking on Vale's masterpiece of a cake.

Back outside, I rested against the wall of the house. The music from the string band floated toward me, a light melody dancing through the deepening darkness. I took a breath. The party was moving along perfectly, and Jules was there, ever-watchful. But still, I needed to get back out there. Dessert was almost ready and I wouldn't miss singing to Vale.

"Elizabeth."

I straightened. Antonio was coming toward me. I went for the kitchen.

"Wait."

I stopped. Maybe he needed something. Something party-related. That was my job after all and I was a professional.

I turned to face him. "Do you need something?"

"Yes." He stopped in front of me. Behind him, lights from the tent emitted a soft glow.

When he didn't say more, I put my hands on my hips, then dropped them. I wasn't there to fight.

"You," he said.

"Excuse me?"

He stepped closer, the toes of his boots dangerously close to the hem of my dress.

"I need you."

I started to shake my head but he placed his fingertips under my chin.

"The party is almost over," he said, his voice low. "We will no longer have a business relationship. I would like to explore another kind of relationship with you now." His fingers moved down my neck and across my collarbone. I shivered.

I stepped back. "No."

Surprise flashed across his face, and hurt. "Don't tell me you don't want this."

I wouldn't tell him that, I couldn't. But. "Your life is complicated. So is mine. I don't think they'd mesh."

His eyebrows lowered. "That is a very flimsy excuse."

"You dismissed me like that," I said, snapping my fingers. "You didn't think twice about it. Like I didn't matter. Not only the work I'd put in, but whatever was starting between us. You didn't bother to explain, or talk to me. You just kicked me out of your house, out of your life."

"Vale—"

"I know you would do anything for her. I would never change that. And if she's uncomfortable with us being together I wouldn't go against her wishes." I fiddled with my neckline. "But you can't use her as an excuse either. You could have talked to me. But you didn't. And I don't need someone like that in my life. I have enough problems trusting someone, letting them in. How can I do that with you, now?"

He ran his hand through his hair.

"I'm sorry, Antonio." I went to walk around him but he placed his hand on my shoulder.

"Please, Elizabeth." His eyes met mine. "You're right. I haven't been with a woman in so long, I've forgotten. I treat everything like business, except Valentina. I considered the loss your company would take when Nita showed up, but I didn't consider your feelings."

"Or it was easier to ignore them."

He nodded. "Maybe."

I studied his face, the lines etched there by time, work, pain. Despite everything, I wanted to smooth those lines, not with Botox or some chemical, but with happiness. I wanted it for him, and I wanted it for me.

"I am sorry," he said. "I should have done things differently."

He started to walk away.

I stomped my foot. "Are you really going to give up that easily?" What I'd said to him was true, I was afraid to let my guard down around him. I was afraid he'd break my heart. But I was also afraid to face a life without him and Vale in it.

He stopped, turned back. His eyebrows rose in a question, in hope, in exasperation.

I stalked closer. "You're not going to fight for me?"

He studied my face, searching for what, an answer?

I moved my lips near his. "You know how I love to fight." I teased him, an almost kiss that he reached for but never caught. "With you especially."

"I'm done fighting." His hands were on me, around me, pulling me in until our bodies were pressed together. His lips took mine, and I gave, willingly. We kissed with an urgency, a need long unfulfilled. My tongue tasted him, spice and heat while his hands roamed in places I'd longed for them to go.

Though I didn't want to, I pulled away. I. Was. A. Professional. And kissing my client's father was *not* professional.

"We both need to get back," I said, my voice breathless. "The cake will be served soon."

He straightened his cape, which had come askew thanks to me. Then he held out his hand. "Shall we?"

I hesitated, a pit dropping into my stomach. "What about Vale?"

He smiled. "Don't worry. She will love the cake."

"No." I shook my head. "Not the cake. Me."

Confusion flickered over his face before he realized what I meant. Or, at least I thought he knew until he said, "It's too complicated, being with a man who has a daughter. I understand."

"Not that." I took the hand that he had retracted. "Vale is everything to you. She has to approve of me. Will she approve of me?"

I hated to admit it, even to myself, but I'd never been more scared of anything in my life. And over what a sixteen-year-old thought.

Antonio nipped at my lips with his. "She approves. Trust me."

I still wasn't sure, but the waiters were carrying out the cake, and we had to rush to follow them so we could sing with the rest of the guests. Antonio stood beside his daughter, his arm around her shoulders as he sang to her. She blew out her candles and everyone clapped.

"Before my dad cuts the cake," Vale said into the mic. "I want to say thank you to everyone for coming, for dressing up, and for making this the best birthday ever."

She turned to me. "Elizabeth. This never would have happened if it weren't for you. You said at the beginning that you would give me exactly what I wanted, and you did. You made a dream I didn't realize I had become reality."

"And to my Dad." She took his hand. "Thank you for being the best dad in the world. I love you."

They hugged as the guests clapped, Antonio whispered something in her ear. When they pulled apart, he sliced the knife through the frosting of the bottom layer. Vale motioned for me and I walked over.

She flung her arms around me. "I can't ever stop saying thank you for this."

"That'll get exhausting," I said and she laughed.

"You're not disappearing now, like you did before."

I swallowed around the lump in my throat. "When the party is over…"

"You're not my fairy godmother," she said. "You're my friend." She hesitated, her face vulnerable. "Right?"

I rolled my eyes with exaggeration. "Obviously."

Antonio's hand slipped around my waist. "And mine too."

Vale glanced between us. Then she rolled her eyes back at me. "Don't say friend, it's weird." She gave her dad a light shove. "You can call her your girlfriend."

Antonio laughed while I felt my face go hot.

"See, I told you she approves," he said.

"Of course I do." Vale leaned toward me and lowered her voice. "Just, take it easy on him, okay? At least sometimes."

"I promise." I arched a brow. "Sometimes."

"I wouldn't have it any other way," Antonio murmured into my ear, causing my whole body to tremble in anticipation.

"You better start passing out that cake," I said, trying to distract myself from where my mind wanted to go, "before people pull out their fake swords."

While Antonio continued to cut the cake, and Vale passed it to her guests, I stood back, watching my masterpiece, AKA the party, continue on. Watching my new future before me in the form of Antonio and Vale. Watching a happiness I couldn't have imagined appear, waiting and within my grasp.

I reached out and took it.

THANK YOU

First, I want to say a huge *thank you* to you. Yes you, the reader of this book! Thank you for reading! An even bigger thank you (like Canada-sized big) if you leave a review. Reviews are so vital and every single one helps. Also, stop by on social media and say hi! I'd love to hear from you. I'm on Facebook, Twitter, Instagram, and my Website.

Thanks to my critique partners: Emily Stanford, Michelle Merrill, and RuthAnne Oakey-Frost. My books would be utter garbage without you amazing ladies.

Even though this book isn't a retelling, it wouldn't be a thing if it weren't for the fabulous Jane Austen. Jane, can I call you Jane? I hope you don't mind that I gave Elizabeth Elliot a happy ending, too.

As always, love and hugs to my family who support me, especially my husband Jeff, and my kids Jade, Logan, Kori, and Avery.

WANT TO READ AVA'S STORY?

SHE'D BE HAPPY TO FORGET...IF THE PAST WOULD JUST STOP HITTING "REPLAY".

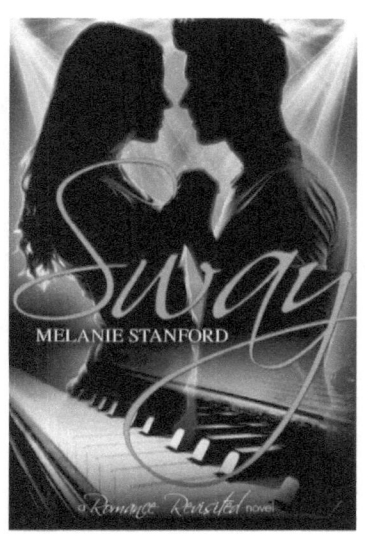

Ava Elliot never thought she'd become a couch surfer. But with a freshly minted—and worthless—degree from Julliard, and her dad squandering the family fortune, what choice does she have?

Living with her old high school friends, though, has its own drawbacks. Especially when her ex-fiancé Eric Wentworth drops back into her life. Eight years ago, she was too young, too scared of being poor, and too scared of her dad's disapproval. Dumping him was a big mistake.

In the most ironic of role reversals, Eric is rolling in musical success, and Ava's starting at the bottom to build her career. Worse, every song Eric sings is an arrow aimed straight for her regrets.

One encounter, one song too many, and Ava can't go on like this. It's time to tell Eric the truth, and make a choice. Finally let go of the past, or risk her heart for a second chance with her first love. If he can forgive her...and she can forgive herself.

Warning: Contains an actor whose kisses taste like chocolate, a pianist with scores of regret, and a sexy crooner who just wants his ex to cry him a river.

Find it everywhere ebooks are sold!

SNEAK PEEK

Read on for a sneak peek of the next

Romance Revisited novel

by Melanie Stanford

COLLIDE

Inspired by Elizabeth Gaskell's classic *NORTH & SOUTH*

Coming soon…

MAGGIE

The sky was a rich blue that belonged over a Van Gogh wheat field, not the lawn in front of Hank's family ranch. The bright sun warmed the bare skin of my arms and legs while a breeze blew into my hair, twirling the ends like silk. But I couldn't breathe.

All of this cloying perfection suffocated me, right down to the plaid blanket I sat on, the wicker basket full of wine and roses, and Hank. Especially Hank, and the four words he had just spoken. Four simple words that sucked the air from my lungs.

It really was a sweet proposal, and I knew Hank thought he was going all out with the picnic and the perfect day, as if he had ordered it all especially. It would've been easy to say yes. In fact, I felt the word at my lips, so close, so ready to slip out, before I swallowed it back down.

Hank knelt across from me, the cowboy hat I thought so sexy in my junior year of high school perched against his knees. He'd ruffled his hair as soon as he took it off to avoid hat head, but all it did was give him a look of wispy childlike innocence. The kind of look that was hard to erase. And yet, all too easy.

"I can't."

His smile froze before it fell altogether. He leaned back on his heels. "What?"

"I'm really sorry," I said, not taking my eyes from his, "but I can't."

"Maggie…" He reached for me, then dropped his hand. "Why?"

I couldn't answer because I didn't know. I'd loved Hank since I was a freshman in high school. Everything about him, from his worn jeans to the dirt under his fingernails and how he masked the smell of horses with Calvin Klein cologne. How he called all women "ma'am," how he could tame the wildest horse and yet every touch on my skin was gentle.

I loved Hank. But I couldn't say yes. It was the "yes" that made it so hard to breathe.

"I'm not ready."

I should have seen this proposal coming. We'd talked of the future lots of times, of being together and living on Hank's family ranch and having kids one day. But it seemed so far off. Unreal. We were only nineteen, after all. It was an adult's life we talked of, and I didn't feel like an adult.

"Then I'll wait. We'll wait." Hank scooted closer, his knees pressed into my thighs. "You can finish community college and by then Dad will let me run the ranch on my own and—"

"No." I couldn't let this go on. This was *his* dream. For a long time it had been my dream too, but I knew in that moment I'd only been borrowing it until I could find my own.

Hank gaped. Then, jamming his hat on his head, he stood and walked away, his shoulders hunching.

"Hank." I followed. "I'm sorry. I really am." I couldn't leave things like this.

He whirled around, brushing my forehead with the brim of his hat. I was taller than Hank without it. The hat gave him height, which is why he wore it all the time, even in church. My dad thought it was sacrilegious but he never made Hank stop.

"You're *sorry*?" His sunburned face had turned a deeper shade of red. "Maggie, we've been dating for *four* years." A puff of air escaped his lips.

The pain he was trying so hard to hide brought tears to my eyes.
"I know."

"This is what comes next." He tipped my chin up with his finger. Hank loved to touch my face, always marveling at my smooth, pale skin compared to his year-round sunburn. "I want it, your parents expect it—"

My eyes narrowed at that, and he quickly changed tack.

"I love you. Don't you love me?"

I swallowed. "I'm sorry." I couldn't explain, couldn't say *I love you*. There was nothing I could do but escape.

Hank followed. He pleaded. He even cried. I cried. He didn't touch me.

"Please don't do this," I said.

The swish of his footsteps behind me died out. He'd finally given up.

"Maggie!" he shouted. "At least let me give you a ride home!"

But I couldn't do that either. I needed to get away from him. Away from myself.

Hank called out again but I ignored him. I didn't stop until I reached the gravel road leading off Hank's family property.

I half expected Hank's pickup to come by, with him hanging out of the window telling me to get in. But he never showed and I was grateful. It was a long walk back into town, but it gave me time. Time to cry, to hate myself, and to think.

A year ago, I graduated high school with a mediocre GPA and a diner job I'd had since I was fourteen. My grades weren't good enough for a top university, so I'd enrolled in the local community college, kept the job where everyone knew my name and gave me crappy tips, and stayed with Hank.

But the whole time I'd had this dream. An alternate life I imagined living when I went to bed at night or while zoning out at the diner.

In this alternate life, I left Hank and Hillstone behind and moved far away —to Las Vegas. I had fabulous friends, a big studio apartment, a job at a trendy boutique, and best of all I danced with Essence Dance Theater, a renowned contemporary dance company I'd seen perform once.

Maybe this alternate life was straight out of a TV show, but I couldn't help wanting something different from what I knew. It's not that I didn't have great friends, because I did. But Drina was at Brown, Stace and her boyfriend were backpacking in Europe, and Melissa had changed her name to Misty and moved to California to be closer to the Mother Ocean, as she called it.

Only I was left, and Hank. Me and Hank. Hank and I. And my parents. Me and Hank and my parents. And his parents and his horses. Me and Hank and my parents and his parents and his horses.

It wasn't enough, yet it was all too much.

My pinkie toes began to sting, the beginnings of blisters. Hillstone was still a mile off. I passed the Williams farm and their pasture of Jersey cows. The same pasture where I'd watched Stace and Melissa/Misty get wasted at Fox Williams' annual New Year's party while I drank a hot chocolate, because my dad would have murdered me if I had even one sip of alcohol. I trudged by the old, rotting barn that everyone said was haunted by headless chickens. I slipped off my sandals as I entered Hillstone, the gravel turning to chipped pavement, hot under my bare feet.

Hillstone was all I knew. It was familiar and safe. Like Hank. But if I couldn't say yes to Hank, I couldn't say yes to Hillstone either.

Maybe it was time to make my daydream a reality.

By the time I got home, the perfect sun was setting in perfect rays of pink and orange. It turned the white siding of my house into the color of Pepto Bismol. I sat on the porch, wrapping my skirt under my legs, unwilling to go inside.

"Maggie?" Mom's voice appeared at my back. "How was your date?"

She knew about the proposal. I could hear it in her voice—the hope, the barely contained excitement.

"We broke up," I said, quick and painless. Just like how I'd refused Hank. Except that hadn't been painless at all.

My mom was by my side in seconds—one of those superhero Mom tricks I figured I'd inherit one day if I ever had kids. I didn't even hear the screen door slam like it always did.

"Honey, why?" Mom put her arm around my shoulders. "What happened?"

I couldn't meet her eyes. "I said no."

Her silence said everything.

I gave her the side eye. "You knew he was going to propose, didn't you?"

She hesitated. "I might have known a thing or two." She pulled my head against her shoulder. "Are you okay?"

"Not really." I'd given up something. I'd given up a life, a future that was certain once, a future I'd set for myself whether I wanted it or not. I couldn't keep living in Hillstone, going to community college, working at the same diner. I wanted to be a different Maggie Hale. I *needed* to be.

It was time for me to try.

ABOUT THE AUTHOR

Melanie Stanford reads too much, plays music too loud, is some-times dancing, and always daydreaming. She would also like her very own TARDIS, but only to travel to the past. She lives outside Calgary, Alberta, Canada with her husband, four kids, and ridicu-lous amounts of snow. Melanie has short stories featured in the Austenesque anthologies THEN COMES WINTER (November 2015) and THE DARCY MONOLOGUES (May 2017).

For More Information:
melaniestanfordbooks.com